ULTIMATE WORLD

ULTIMATE

WORLD

HUGO GERNSBACK

Edited, with an introduction

by SAM MOSKOWITZ

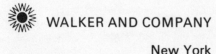 WALKER AND COMPANY

New York

First published in the United States of America in 1971 by the Walker Publishing Company, Inc.

Published simultaneously in Canada by Fitzhenry & Whiteside, Limited, Toronto.

ISBN: 0-8027-5542-9

Library of Congress Catalog Card Number: 73-161119

Designed by Carl Weiss and Robert Hansell

Printed in the United States of America.

C782972

CONTENTS

Introduction

THE

ULTIMATE

HUGO

GERNSBACK

By Sam Moskowitz

Hugo Gernsback occupies the same position in relation to the history of science fiction as George Washington does in relation to the history of the United States. There was a land, a government and a people on this continent long before 1776, just as there was science fiction published long before 1926. The thirteen colonies were not an independent nation before 1776 and might not have become so without George Washington, and there were no science fiction magazines before 1926 and their existence can be credited completely to Hugo Gernsback. That is why, just as

George Washington is called by the historians of the United States "the father of our country," Hugo Gernsback is called by literary historians "the father of science fiction."

Hugo Gernsback has earned another great distinction in the field of science fiction beyond that as its inaugural publisher in a genre magazine. In a literary form, whose brightest aspect is prophecy, he stands in the front rank as one of the greatest prophets of them all. His reputation for this gift rests primarily in the content of (until now) his only published novel, *Ralph 124C 41+*. This novel, originally published serially in his magazine *Modern Electrics* (April, 1911, to March, 1912), must certainly rank as one of the greatest fictional works of technological prophecy ever published. Probably the only other single work that deserves comparison with *Ralph 124C 41+* is Albert Robida's personally illustrated *Twentieth Century,* published in France in 1883. That volume with its concepts of jet planes, radio, automats, submarines, television, poison and germ warfare, deserves respect. Gernsback excelled in his sound, scientific explanation of how his prophecies would come into being. The most striking example was his accurate description of the principles of what is today called radar and his diagram of the "mirror," which catches the microwaves reflected from metal in their path. Equally accurate were his predictions of television (including closed-circuit) and the very name television itself, which he introduced to the United States. While space travel was a part of his book, even more amazing were its less grandiose speculations of tape recorders, loudspeakers, juke boxes, fluorescent lighting, vending machines dispensing hot and cold foods and innumerable other technical and social innovations that have since become part of our civilization.

He published the first radio magazine in the world, *Modern Electrics,* in 1908 and this magazine evolved into *The Electrical Experimenter* in 1914 and finally *Science and Invention* from 1920 on. During this entire period, it was Hugo Gernsback's job, as editor and publisher, to create original and scientifically plausible ideas of future advances or novel adaptations of existing technology. The parade of ideas was endless: weather control, wireless transmission of power, flying tanks, space probes, automated cities, solar power, glass skyscrapers, radio and television networks, medical diagnosis by radio and television, tear gas for quelling mobs, organ transplants, helicopter buses, jet planes, voice prints, electronic music —literally thousands of concepts.

It was in his marketing of many science fiction publications that he realized the limitations of the speculative article. The slogan carried on the title page of his magazine *Science and Invention,* a quote from Thomas Huxley: "Those Who Refuse to Go Beyond Fact Rarely Get as Far as Fact," was in reality a reply to critics.

The August, 1923, issue of his magazine *Science and Invention* was a landmark in the history of science fiction inasmuch as it emblazoned on the cover "Scientific Fiction Number," and portrayed a space-suited figure painted by Howard V. Brown, illustrating G. Peyton Wertenbaker's story, *The Man From the Atom.* There were five other illustrated stories of "scientific fiction," including one by Hugo Gernsback himself. In his editorial for that issue entitled *Predicting Future Inventions* Hugo Gernsback made a revealing statement: "There are a certain class of people, and we hear continually from them, who condemn the policy of this magazine because we exploit the future. These good people never realize that there can be no progress without prediction. It is impossible to have in mind an invention without planning it beforehand, and no matter how fantastic and impossible the device may appear, there is no telling when it will attain reality in the future."

Hugo Gernsback had been running science fiction in his periodicals ever since he began serialization of *Ralph 124C 41+*. He regarded fiction as a prime method of dramatizing the application of a scientific advance which at that date might purely be in the imagination. This belief was fortified by reader reaction.

Gernsback's fondness for scientific ideas expressed in fictional form can be traced back to his youth. He was born in Luxembourg August 16, 1884, son of a Jewish wine wholesaler, and received a good scientific education in Ecole Industrielle of Luxembourg and the Technikum in Bingen, Germany. The language of his youth was German, though he read and spoke English and French.

He was technically oriented from his early childhood and in his teens gained a small reputation for his knowledge of electricity. He invented a layer battery capable of three times the current output of any similar unit then in existence. He eventually left Europe because he could not obtain a patent there for his battery. But there was also a literary and romantic side to his nature that would eventually be reconciled by promotion of science through *fiction,* and this resulted in the world's first science fiction magazine, *Amazing Stories,* April, 1926.

Until now, there has been nothing in print concerning his first unpublished novel, written at the age of seventeen in German, the original typescript of which is in my possession. It is about 62,000 words long and titled *Ein Pechvogel*. "Pechvogel" is a term used in derision, somewhat comparable to the Yiddish "schlemiel," which describes an impractical person for whom everything turns out wrong, no matter how well-intentioned, because of his lack of common sense.

Because of his advocacy of science, because of Prussian-like formal appearance (even to the point of screwing on a monocle when reading menus), and because he did not permit many people to get to know him closely, few realized that humor ranked second only to science as Hugo Gernsback's great love. He liked all kinds of humor, whether broad corn, subtly sophisticated wit, slapstick, puns, play on words, anagrams or bizarre situations. In his technical magazines, at least 50 percent of all the stories he ran were humor. There were marvelous opportunities for slapstick fun in an inventor's new creation gone wild, and Gernsback reveled in them. He brought Ellis Parker Butler to *Radio News* to write a series of funny scientific stories based on radio, a number of them straight science fiction. He himself wrote a long series of new adventures of Baron Munchausen on Mars, and printed endlessly the unfortunate and funny "Scientific Adventures of Mr. Fosdick" by the ingenious Jacques Morgan, a businessman who wrote them for fun and eschewed payment. He ran a truly zany series of Henry Hugh Simmons in the early *Amazing Stories* under the general heading of "Hicks' Inventions With a Kick."

The pioneer science fiction magazine artist, Frank R. Paul, suited Gernsback particularly, because Paul had extensive experience as a cartoonist on *The Jersey Journal,* and could come through with the madcap sort of illustrations that were needed to express the mood of these stories.

In late 1927 and early 1928, Gernsback issued a weekly magazine *French Humor* composed of both cartoons and jokes, reprinted from the French with English translations below the French. Extremely novel was *Tidbits,* a monthly humor magazine which contained such departments as News Blunders, Phoney Patents, Advertwisters, Radiocrostics, Namystics and Cookoo Nuts. The last mentioned was a Gernsback invention of which he was particularly proud. It consisted of taking a famous saying or popular expression and with artwork warping it in some hopefully humorous fashion. For example: "Holy Smoke" would be illustrated by a picture of a church burning; "She rolls her own," shows a woman wheeling a baby in a carriage or "Amazing Stories" finds a man gaping up at a tremendous skyscraper. Readers were asked to send in their Cookoo Nuts and cash prizes from one to three dollars were offered for those selected. Their popularity was great enough to encourage Gernsback to issue in magazine format the *Cookoo Nuts Book* in 1928. When he published *Superworld Comics,* beginning in April, 1940, he ran Cookoo Nuts as a feature of that magazine. The reaction from the kids was so favorable that he issued a single issue of *Cookoo Nuts* dated March, 1941, as a separate publication.

He was involved in a number of one shot humor magazines including *1,001 Laughs* (1927), *Oi! Oi! I'm Leffing,* a compendium of Jewish humor published in 1928, *Snappy Humor* (1929), *Favorite Jokes of Famous People* (1930) and was early in the comic book business with *Smatter Pop* an octavo-sized collection of the daily strips from the once-famous comic of the same name which he issued in 1928.

During the forties and fifties Hugo Gernsback would turn out elaborate "Christmas Cards," which were digest-sized parodies and lampoons of famous publications, running up to 48 pages in size with four-colored covers and two-color illustrations.

Humor—any kind of humor—was part of Gernsback

from his earliest youth until the day of his death. This puts into focus that little-known early novel *Ein Pechvogel,* authored by "von Huck Gernsbacher." Why "Huck?" Because as a boy Hugo Gernsback's favorite author along with Jules Verne was Mark Twain, and of Twain's books he was fondest of *Huckleberry Finn.* Therefore, when he wrote his first novel, and that first novel turned out to be slapstick humor almost in the style of the soon-to-be-popularized Hollywood short comedies, he felt that "Huck Gernsbacher" expressed the mood of the piece.

The novel is written in the first person and the action takes place in England. The lead character is Tom Bouggerton, whom the famous saying "the road to Hell is paved with good intentions," might have memorialized. At his university class, chemicals are added to chalk so that when the professor uses it, red chalk writes green and white chalk, blue. When blamed for the transposition, he remains quiet, rather than squeal.

While conducting a chemistry experiment, he almost blows himself up, cutting his ear, and is expelled from the University.

While training for a hunt he accidentally kills his neighbor's dog. When in disgust he takes the bullets from his gun, he is unable to defend himself and a girl against a sudden attack by a boar and undignifiedly must scramble up to the heights.

When he proposes to a girl in a dark garden, he finds he has expressed his ardent desires to the wrong person.

He tries his hand at writing a novel. Since he had typed on both sides of the sheet of paper he finds that the manuscript must be retyped. He does so and throws away the original. The publisher loses his manuscript and he is out of luck.

He then decides to conduct an experiment in applied

psychology by putting his hand on the shoulder of a stranger and saying: "You are under arrest!" A cop sees the act and takes the two of them into custody. The stranger he has tapped avers that Bouggerton is an accomplice in an hotel theft. When, in desperation, Bouggerton tells the truth in order to save himself, he is slapped with the charge of impersonating an officer.

There are an endless series of incidents involving business, love and friendship where Bouggerton can never seem to do anything right, and the novel gradually descends into almost absurd slapstick. However, there are two sequences which are harbingers of the Hugo Gernsback of the future.

One of the most fascinating is a venture in which our "hero" begins an enterprise in which the sun's rays or solar energy is used to roast coffee. This reduces the cost of coffee so much that the idea is an enormous success and a second plant is contemplated. Inevitably, one morning it rains, and the weakness in the method is apparent. His partner attempts to utilize heat lamps on those days when there is inadequate sunlight, but it continues to rain. Finally, orders are turned over to another company to keep customers during periods of inadequate sunlight. But soon, a roasted coffee appears on the market at a price lower than the best they can produce. Their process has been stolen and taken to the Sahara Desert where the sunlight never fails and where patent laws of England do not apply.

He finally sells his process to a southern United States company for the first real money he has ever known. With this money he quite appropriately organizes a club of unlucky "schlemiels," who gather to tell one another their various misfortunes.

The club members claim that Alexander the Great was one with them in spirit, because he took a bath in cold water and died.

The clubhouse is built of iron and cement to protect it against fire, but the iron draws a bolt of lightning and the clubhouse is demolished. The club membership is heir to such atrocious luck that it is impossible to hold the group together.

There is one other business that our hero enters which is of scientific interest. He builds an umbrella-vending machine, from which an umbrella may be procured upon the deposit of a coin. Some of the money is automatically returned when the umbrella is put back into the machine. The scheme fails when dishonest people return their broken umbrellas for the deposit money.

The novel ends in a fiasco in which our hero is accidentally separated from his wife in Brussels, and searches for her in several countries. It concludes when he tells his friends that he has found her, but it is obvious that his woes are to continue in perpetuity. He is one of the hapless people of the world.

Hugo Gernsback was also a magazine pioneer in that he presented sex as popular educational material.

There had been material on sexual problems in magazines like Bernarr McFadden's *Physical Culture,* but they were usually of so generalized a nature as to present nothing more than the "thrill" of knowing that one was reading about a delicate subject. Hugo Gernsback started in 1928 a handsomely printed quarterly *Your Body,* with the sub-title of "Know Thyself." He secured a group of medical doctors who either supplied editorial direction or were contributors, among them the science fiction writer David H. Keller, M.D. The publication was a quality effort and contained a cross-section of material on hygiene, biology, medicine, beauty culture, health and sex of such general interest and excellence that after more than 40 years, they still make fascinating and informative reading.

Every issue of the magazine contained a selection of articles under the heading of "Sex Problems," and a genuine attempt was made to solve them. Cross-sections of sex organs were presented, and the mechanics of reproduction rarely seen in hardcover books, let alone in magazines, were explained.

In 1928, Hugo Gernsback under his Popular Book Corporation imprint, published a 10-volume, hardcover set called *Sexual Education Series* written by David H. Keller, M.D. The 10 volumes sold for $3.50, and in 1930 were revised and reprinted in an impressive 50-cent volume, flat-sized and paperbound under the title of *Know Yourself!* "Mysteries of Life Explained," by David H. Keller, M.D.

Hugo Gernsback's most courageous enterprise was the founding of a digest-sized monthly in 1933 titled *Sexology,* an educational self-help magazine on sex, written and edited by medical men. It presented answers to important questions and alleviated potential suffering and tragedy brought about by ignorance. Today, it is still being published in Spanish and English, and many of its "shocking" subjects are regular fare in *Reader's Digest, McCall's, Look, Life* and *Ladies Home Journal.*

The most serious trouble *Sexology* experienced during its long history was when it ran an article consisting of a series of quotes relating to sex from the Old Testament. There was no commentary, merely quotes. Hugo Gernsback was asked to pay a visit to the U.S. Attorney General shortly after the appearance of the magazine.

"Mr. Gernsback," he was told, "we are familiar with your magazine and have been ever since it began publication. We consider it suitable matter to be carried through the mails of the United States and feel it is performing a useful service. However, your piece on sex in the Bible has gotten us so many complaints from the clergy of all denominations that we may have to take action unless you promise not to reprint anything from the Holy Scriptures again!"

"But," explained Gernsback, "we added no comment of any sort, we merely quoted from the Bible."

"I know. But if you will give me your word to keep the Bible out of your magazine, I think I can promise you that there will be no trouble from us."

"And that was the closest I ever came to being accused of publishing pornography," Hugo Gernsback added, on telling this author the story.

Ultimate World is a product of Hugo Gernsback's later years, and as such is a combination of science fiction, humor and sex homogenized in a delightful manner made possible by maturity. This is not a novel of his youth, such as *Ein Pechvogel*, dug out of an old trunk and offered only because of the fame of the author. *Ultimate World* was written in large part in 1958 and completed in early 1959.

It might, then, be readily and reasonably asked, if the novel was so interesting, why has it not been published in the years between its completion and now? The answer is simple. In the form in which Hugo Gernsback first submitted it, it was interposed with non-fiction essays that almost doubled its length.

As he received early rejections, he agreed to trim down *some* of the non-fiction material, but it wasn't until after his death, August 19, 1967, that I went through the novel and excised everything that was not fiction and had an editor read it on that basis.

Many of Gernsback's editorials, articles and essays were individually stimulating, but the best way to present them would be as a separate book and some publisher may someday decide to do just that.

What remains, then, is a book with mind-invigorating ideas which go far beyond those presented in *Ralph 124C 41+* and add another dimension to Hugo Gernsback as a prophet. *Ultimate World* is destined to become a new source book for science fiction plots.

To date, only one other man, Philip José Farmer has nearly as successfully used the *science* of sex as the basis for strong science fiction.

This book also strikes a telling blow at the false human vanity displayed in much science fiction. It indicates just how helpless we would be against a truly advanced race. How we would have difficulty comprehending their motives, making sense of their methods or even copying their science.

The book is far more than a compendium of new ideas. It is a book with a deep social message, presented with situations that immediately arouse and sustain curiosity.

Humor lightens the book all the way. For example, "Popoff's Ordeal," in Chapter Four, is little short of hilarious, but the reader is aware that his ideas are not to be lightly dismissed.

The problem of the parents in controlling the children in Chapter Thirteen is chilling in view of what is happening today. If you think the world has problems with a "Generation Gap," read Hugo Gernsback.

Ultimate World is a highly original and entertaining book conveying a message of emphatic importance. It is written well and reads easily. It may prove to be controversial and probably will be praised and damned to excess, but it should eventually command as much respect for its soundly based prophetic imagination as the early *Ralph 124C 41+*. In addition it deserves recognition for its outspoken social criticism.

1

THE

HOUSE

TORNADO

They were sitting on their sumptuous *tempreg* (temperature regulated) foamplastic couch opposite the fireplace. Above it the normally beautiful crystal mirror had, by the flick of a switch, become an illuminated chessboard with its thirty-two chessmen. The two players, each holding a miniature chessgame in his hands, watched the large board over the fireplace intently. As each player moved a pawn or other piece on his hand-board, the corresponding move on the large illuminated board followed electronically. Had there been company, everyone could have watched the progress of the game from all over the room.

But that memorable night they were alone—Duke Dubois, famed professor of physics at Columbia

University, and his wife, Donny, beautiful and sensuous ex-haute couture model and daughter of Auguste Hawthorne, dean of the School of Engineering at Columbia.

Professor Dubois, an inventor of note, was at home in practically any branch of science, including sexology. A Nobel prizewinner for his recent discovery, the *Cosmitronic Field Theory*, he had won worldwide fame at the age of thirty-six. The couple lived in a large two-storey stone and marble villa in a secluded spot on the Palisades overlooking the Hudson, in New Jersey. The house was crammed with Dubois' own devices and inventions—from the tempreg couch to the *electronichess* over the mantelpiece.

Dubois, who had patented a one-man *cosmiflyer* (a six-inch cosmic power generator which is strapped to the back and operates like a rocket without a hot exhaust), was accustomed to fly directly from his home over the Hudson to the University, returning in the same manner evenings.

The couple, much to their regret, had no children.

It was 2330 when Dubois and his wife went to bed that night. Reclining on their *auto bedprop,* they were watching the late *Color Picture News* as it flashed on the large bedroom mirror when, without warning, the dateline, June 24, 1996, the picture, sound and news all disappeared together. Simultaneously, a small tornado roared into the bedroom from the open west and south windows. The flimsy nightgown of Duke's wife was neatly ripped off her and disappeared through the west window, leaving her completely nude. Duke, wearing the latest style one-piece *abrijama* fared better—at least he stayed dressed.

He immediately noted that his normal weight of 170 pounds had almost vanished and that the tornado-like wind was not the reason. He and Donny held on desperately to the top of the bed while all sorts of light household objects sailed past them, some of them colliding painfully with their bodies. Donny's array of perfume bottles seemed to explode as the glass stoppers, popping like champagne corks in the rarefied air, sucked the perfume out in colored, miniature comet-like tails which disappeared through the window.

Duke and Donny had a hard time breathing. Their bodies by now were floating horizontally while they were still frantically clutching the top of the bed. Donny's screams sounded faintly in the tornado's roaring blast, as did Duke's shouted encouragements.

"The house must be in a near-weightless, negative-gravitational field," he yelled. "I can't weigh more than 20 pounds. There are some 20,000 cubic feet of air in the house that normally weigh 1,600 pounds . . . but now weigh only 150 or 160 pounds. Heavy new outside air is being sucked in with a weight difference of some 1,400 pounds. . . . That creates the tornado, since the lighter air is pushed out violently."

While he spoke, the air suddenly calmed down and both Donny and Duke sank gently, like two falling leaves, exhausted on their large double bed. Duke, always the man of science, suddenly jumped from his reclining position, but instantly regretted the move, as his head collided with the ceiling. Ruefully rubbing his forehead, he slowly landed on his feet, then cautiously made his way to the bathroom. He stepped on his spring scale and said:

"See, what I said is right. I weigh exactly 18 pounds, just 10 percent of my 180 pounds weight!" He gingerly picked up his featherweight wife and placed her on the scale.

"Well, what do you say now? You won't have to reduce anymore—a scant 13 pounds, just about 10 percent of your old weight!"

Unaccustomed to their new and lighter weight, they

groped their way to the window over the litter of household paraphernalia cluttering the floor. The usual street scene was no longer in evidence—neither lawn nor trees nor sidewalk.

Instead, they looked with wonder on a dense purplish haze or fog, quite impenetrable to their eyes. Slowly they picked their way through the other rooms on the floor, past broken mirrors, pictures hanging at crazy angles, torn lamp shades, demolished glassware and bric-a-brac. The view through the other windows was the same—a dense, purple haze. Out on the porch, which was also a shambles, Duke took a few steps toward the haze, then hastily withdrew.

"Damn if it isn't charged!" he exclaimed excitedly. "I can't get near it—even at this distance I'm tingling all over. It must be a force-field of tremendous energy. This certainly is exciting—I never encountered the like of it in physics." After a little pause, "Shades of Einstein, it looks as if we've been kidnapped! Let's get back to the bedroom, quick!"

There he dialed the operator, but got only a loud static roar and a faint busy signal. He then tried to call his father in Hoboken, N.J., then the New York *Times,* then Columbia University—but all lines were uniformly roaring and busy. He doubted that he could have been able to carry on an intelligible conversation even if his party had answered.

Dejected, both he and Donny sat down on their bed.

"Do you think we're still on Earth?" ventured Donny, white and trembling and still quite nude.

Duke laughingly soothed her with a kiss and explained, "We're still on terra firma; otherwise the phone line would be cut. You noticed that when I turned on the hot water a few minutes ago, it still worked as usual. Also, since all our house lights are *atomelectronic,* they are self-contained and don't depend on outside current. And, as you observed, our Color Picture News is out, so there's little use trying our other electronic communications—they'll be out, too."

So saying, he switched on in turn the city *telibrary*, the *teletheater* (live from San Francisco's *Orpheum*), the *telunar space show* (live from the moon's interior)—but there was only a shattering roar on all the channels, just as he suspected would happen.

While he was still talking, first Donny, then Duke faintly noted a somewhat peculiar pungent, musky scent. Gradually it became stronger. It was indescribably soothing, yet tingling to the senses. As Donny analyzed it later, it had a powerful aphrodisiac quality that inexplicably aroused her. Duke immediately divined its purpose: it had an extremely powerful effect on his spinal nerves and erotogenic centers. The tumescent effect was overpowering and within seconds, he as well as Donny dismissed their recent extraordinary experiences and everything else from their minds except animal passion. Duke ripped off his abrijamas and flung himself passionately at the nude form of his wife in a marital union such as humanity had never experienced before. Days later he was to make these notes of his experiences.

DUBOIS' NOTES

Ever since the advent of the human race, man had been chained securely to his gravity-dominated planet. Even standing for any length of time was tiring. Lying down was not always restful, particularly if one was overweight. Being thin was not helpful, either, because the necessary energy, muscular and nervous, was usually deficient.

During marital union, since the average male weighed 170 pounds and his mate 125, the couple was quickly exhausted, chiefly because of their weight. More so in the hot seasons.

When couples were overweight, marital intercourse generally became unsatisfying to both. This was particularly true with the male in the superior position.

Sexologists have been contending for ages that there is no new thing under the sun in sex. It is literally true that nothing new in sexual relations between the sexes has been experienced in thousands of years. The ancient East Indians, in their famed temples of Kranach, Bharat, Konarak, Orissa, Khajurado and others, left us their fabulous sculptures, as part of their phallic worship, in every imaginable sexual position and junction.

Space flight, for the first time since the beginning of humanity, added a new dimension to sex expression—weightlessness.

During the pioneering years of space flight, when unmanned rocket ships and later manned *atomflight* came into use, man had no opportunity for actual conjugal relations in spaceships. Indeed, during the early exploration flights to the moon, only male crews were allowed and of these a large percentage perished. Even when the first moon flights with standard *atomtransports* were inaugurated in 1975, passengers still had to be strapped to their seats to avoid "weightlessness chaos." This condition is true even today and will remain so until 1999, when we will have our first cabin-equipped transports, according to *Translunar Space Lines.* Up to then, there will be no private space cabins, hence no "free fall"—weightless honeymoon en route to the moon.

According to the current 1996 *Space Almanac,* it was Col. George Adamos, of the U.S. Atomic Forces, and his wife, Frances, who experienced the first and historic human marital intercourse of partial weightlessness in 1977 on the moon. But as a human weighing 150 pounds on earth weighs 24-3/4 pounds on the moon, the weight is still considerable. He described his experiences in detail in *U.S. Space Medicine* for Dec. 1977, pointing out that the energy output during even vigorous intercourse is greatly lowered on the moon. He called attention to the fact that this is of great importance to elderly people and, particularly, to cardiac (heart) cases, who should be greatly benefited by several months' stay on the moon.

It was also in that magazine article that Col. Adamos made his now famous historic remark: *"When man has finally conquered gravity and has experienced total weightlessness, then and then only will fortunate lovers taste fully the exquisite fruits of the gods, when, released from the ancient gravitational chains while floating in free and caressing space, they are joined in ecstatic bliss."*

* * *

That Donny and I should be one of the first humans to experience marital bliss in total weightlessness was, in a way, no great surprise. After we had weighed ourselves that memorable night of June 24-25, 1996, and found our weights to be 13 pounds and 18 pounds respectively, I expected almost anything. During our ensuing induced marital conjunctions, we suddenly found ourselves floating free in space, directly above our bed. Whoever for the moment was directing our destiny had reduced the gravity of our house and its contents to zero. It occurred to me that the purple haze-wall prevented all air motion for the time being, and for that reason there was little disturbance of objects. But we, the two humans on the bed, were in full marital kinetic motion. As we now had zero weight, the slightest reaction projected us away from the bed's surface into the air above.

We tumbled delightfully about the room, clutched tightly together in the most grotesque positions. We bumped into walls and ceilings, but in a few seconds learned to ward off collisions with hands or feet. As we weighed nothing, we did not have to expend the usual laborious muscular effort; hence the session lasted far longer and was much less exhausting than in full gravity. Here both of us must confess that we completely lost track of all passage of time. We have no clear idea when we first embraced and when we ended this extraordinary and so altogether exhilarating and satisfying experience. However, we now know that the love accouplement must have lasted for at least one full hour.

We finally drew apart—still in mid-air—and by deft, acrobatic maneuvering regained the surface of the bed for a short rest. Such is lifelong habit that we did not at once realize that in zero gravitation, a bed is only a hindrance, which at best only heats the body where it contacts the bedsheet. Hence we soon floated upward once more, a feat which was accomplished by the merest pressure of a finger against the bed. We were now floating, separated by less than a foot. As we were stretched out and rigid, we soon hung motionless in space, but imperceptibly, little by little, under the laws of universal gravitation, the masses of our bodies exerted their mutual attraction on each other and soon we were in physical contact again. But just as this occurred, the pungent aphrodisiac odor permeated the air once more, with the original result.

This time, a vague suspicion, which had formed slowly, became a certainty.

"Donny," I whispered excitedly, "we are being forced to perform and are under observation by some alien and diabolical super-intelligence. We must have been under continuous and minute investigation ever since this started."

"But what can we do?" This in her dreamy and no longer alarmed voice. "Besides, this is a much too wonderful experience—let them!"

Normally, my extremely prim and correct wife would have been horrified and would have recoiled from being spied on during what she calls "life's most sacred moments." Yet under the powerful effect of the mysterious sexological emanation, the normal defenses of both of us were completely paralyzed. Pure, stark animal desire possessed us so overwhelmingly that it drove everything else from our consciousness.

Once more for a long time, we found ourselves in paradise, oblivious to everything. This was repeated several more times during the night until, finally exhausted—and gradually becoming resentful against the alien, superior force—we fell into a beneficial sleep.

It was nine o'clock when we woke, somewhat confused and "beat up," as one feels after an extended orgy. All muscles and ligaments were aching in both of us after the unusual activity we had undergone. Despite our extraordinarily delightful experiences, never even imagined before, the inevitable reaction set in and we were soon boiling-angry. We fumed, we snarled like two wounded animals. I shook my fist at the invisible entity that had degraded us; I swore as I never had before. Donny, hysterical and screaming, battered the mattress with both fists in an explosion of anger and resentment.

This was but the natural result of our hurt and bruised pride, our dignity as humans, vented against our captors who had treated us as if we were trained fleas.

Suddenly, realizing the futility of our exhibition and divining that we were still under surveillance, we sobered completely and looked sheepishly at each other.

"Gravitation fully restored," I noted. "They must have turned it on very gradually while we slept, otherwise there would have been a reverse tornado."

"Yes," said Donny, "these unspeakable creatures restored the full air pressure at the same time, I think. And it's getting hot; that damned purple haze is still there, too."

"Yes, it looks as if we are still held captive—I wonder how long we will be under compulsive observation."

I walked over and closed the windows and snapped on the glass-pane *tempconditioners*.* I noticed that the electronic glass became frosty as usual, which meant that the wiring to the house atompower plant in the basement was still connected and functioning.

"We'd better have breakfast," I ordered Donny, grumpishly. "We both are as hungry as a swarm of locusts after that enforced 'labor of love . . .' "

"Good God," Donny interrupted suddenly, while making breakfast, with a wild look at me, "you don't think they'll turn on that sex-incense, or whatever that devilishness is, once more!"

"No use fighting against it—they probably will, and there's nothing we can do about it!"

"But can't we rig up some exhaust or blower?"

"No, that wouldn't work. We're surrounded with some sort of airtight enclosure—see that purplish wall—and *all* the air we breathe will be permeated with any drug or emanation

---

*Tempconditioners are electronic, non-mechanical air-conditioning appliances. They are made of porous transparent glass that is also a semiconductor. It absorbs moisture from the air and cools the air simultaneously.

they inject into it."

"But suppose we dress fully, me with my elastic panty girdle, you with your winter underwear—anything, so we don't have to go through that degrading forced performance again . . . I am satiated . . . the very thought of sex makes me scream."

"Darling," I sighed, "since last night you have felt only a very miniscule fraction of this alien entity's power. From what little we have experienced, I suspect that the intelligence of our captors must be millions of years ahead of our civilization; hence I am certain that they can make us do *anything* they wish. Incidentally, when we come under the influence of the—let's call it *insexence,* again, I know that in no time flat we shall be compelled to undress and obey their will. I am so certain of their superior intelligence that there seems no use fighting against it.

"Right now we're like a captured anthill in a scientist's well-equipped laboratory. We are the silly, helpless ants, studied by the entomologist, who learns all about our behavior, our biological structure, our mating habits, our life cycle and anything else he—or they—want to know."

"But," Donny ventured, "why don't we see our captors, and why don't they talk with us, or at least communicate with us?"

For some reason, this question made me laugh uproariously. "Don't be silly; have you ever heard of a scientist who communicated with an ant or talked to their queen? With its restricted vision, an ant has never seen a human, certainly not in its full perspective. And why should a human want to communicate with an ant? They've done it in science fiction, but serious scientists have no way of reaching the 'mentality' of an ant, even knowing their social organization is over 50 million years ahead of ours. There is a good possibility that ants for their part may have tried to communicate with us for millions of years, but we are too ignorant, or haven't the tools or senses to intercept their messages—if there are any.

"You must understand that humans are late, newcomer-freaks on this earth and still have lots to learn."

There was a long pause while we wolfed down the equivalent of four breakfasts. Finally Donny, fingering her throat, whispered, awestruck, "Do you think that this . . . they . . . whoever they are, came from outer space?"

"Before I can give an intelligent answer to that, I must have much more information about them. We don't as yet know exactly what they are after; whether they are friendly and merely wish to study us, or whether they are hostile and have come to subjugate the entire earth, our lives and our institutions. *Anything* is possible. They may come from the far depths of space, they may come from an entirely different time-dimension from ours, they may come from an adjacent hyper-space, or from an interatomic world. We know so little of our multifaceted, illimited universe that the most impossible conjecture today becomes commonplace tomorrow."

I had not finished my sentence when we both heard a strange series of noises on the floor, still littered with debris. As we watched spellbound, we saw broken pieces of a large vase and glass splinters from a mirror and various other demolished objects rejoin themselves in mid-air as if by magic. It was as if we were looking at a movie running in reverse. In far less time than it takes to tell about it, every object that had been broken or destroyed had been *rematerialized* as if it had never been broken! But for a fraction of a second just after the pieces had been fitted together, there was a momentary blur, as if the object had been whisked away. More inexplicable, during that vanishing moment, the vases, all bric-a-brac, mirrors, lamp shades—in short, *everything* broken or torn—had been whisked back in place, completely restored and replaced where it had been before the house-tornado.

We had watched this superperformance that took only a few seconds with fascinated, openmouthed wonder and disbelief.

"Now, how in the world—it just can't be!" gasped Donny.

It took me a while to collect my senses, but suddenly I thought I had the answer.

"Not so impossible as it looks; it's been anticipated for a long time, ever since the old days of wireless.* In 1909, a scientist described how solids could be dematerialized and

*See "Wireless on Mars," *Modern Electrics* magazine, Feb., 1909, page 394.

sent through space by means of radio waves. At the receiving end, the solids (or liquids) were rematerialized once more. That is the process—probably much improved—which you just witnessed. Evidently our superintelligent captors are not only superorderly but also move like lightning!"

End of Dubois' notes

Dubois and his wife were still sitting at the breakfast table when they felt a slight shaking of the house. Simultaneously, brilliant sunshine broke through the windows for the first time since their "capture." They rushed out on the porch and saw that the purple haze had vanished. Hundreds of people in the street surged forward toward them. Photographers and reporters suddenly assaulted their house in a solid phalanx. Hastily throwing on dressing gowns, they allowed some twenty shouting people inside, all reporters and photographers. Outside there was pandemonium.

2

THE

10-BALLS

A hush fell on the reporters and photographers when Otto Salzbrecht of the New York *Times,* dean of New York's newsmen, cleared his throat and respectfully addressed the distinguished couple.

"Professor Dubois, allow me to hand you your two undelivered copies of my paper, which I found on your outside letterbox. We know you have had no news for the past two days, and . . ."

Dubois leaped from his chair and almost tore the papers from the reporter's hand. He looked at the dates, June 25 and 26, and sank bewildered into his chair. He passed his hand over his forehead and glanced strangely at his wife. The reporters looked questioningly at each other, sensing something extraordinary. They were not mistaken.

"Ladies and gentlemen," said Dubois in a strained and tired voice, "we have gone through a vast assortment of extraordinary experiences in a short length of time. But the latest one, which you just gave us, is perhaps most significant."

The reporters and photographers stared uncomprehendingly as Dubois continued.

"When we woke up at 9:00 A.M. this morning, we were quite certain that our trials began *last night,* but now we find that our adventure began the day before yesterday. Somehow there is a whole day for which we cannot account. True, we were ravenously hungry on awakening, but it seemed to us that we had slept only a few short hours. It now appears as if our captors experimented on us for a full twenty-four hours while we were completely unconscious—or else we were transported into an entirely alien space-time continuum for some incomprehensible purpose. Whatever experiences we had in those twenty-four lost hours were completely blotted out from our memories. Perhaps our captors don't want us to know too much! It's most bewildering and sinister in its implications."

There was a pause and a great deal of excited murmuring. Then once more reporter Salzbrecht spoke:

"Professor, will you please give us a full report of your experiences to bring us up to date? We know what's going on *outside,* but we know little of the *inside.*"

"In a moment," said Dubois, "but first I must have an inkling of who or what our captors are."

"I wish we could tell you," sighed Salzbrecht, "but we are as puzzled as you. All we know is that on the evening of June 24 at 2330 New York time, the earth was invaded by probably a thousand *10-Balls* which spread over the whole globe."

"10-Balls? What are they?" queried Dubois in a puzzled voice.

"They are huge affairs as big as a twenty-five storey apartment house. The machines—if they are machines—are made up of three tiers of large spheres. The lower tier has six balls, the second three balls, and the top a single ball, twice as large as the others. They are made of a mirror-like, silvery substance. There are no windows visible anywhere. Strangest of all, *there are no connections or supports between the balls*—they all seem to float free, like giant electrons in an atomic diagram.

"But from the top ball a hazy, purplish tube extends down below the level of the lowest ball-tier. It was this tube that descended and covered your house, while the rest of the machine floated about 300 feet or thereabouts above your villa. Normally, the machines stay at an approximate 1,500-foot level."

"A hazy purple tube that descended over our house, somewhat like the *ovipositor* of a female insect," mused Dubois, lost in thought momentarily. "I presume no government or commercial communication agencies picked up any special signals," he said aloud.

"None whatsoever," affirmed Salzbrecht, "nor did the 10-Balls respond to any of ours, sent over a wide range of radio frequencies."

"I had a vague inkling of this," said Dubois with a knowing look at his wife.

He then gave a twenty-minute resumé of their weird experiences, stating all the facts in short, clipped sentences, just as if he were giving a lecture at Columbia. To questions of what he thought of the invaders, where they originated, and what their real purpose was on earth, Dubois gave the same answers he had given his wife that morning.

"Have there been any attacks on us, or did we attack their machines?" Dubois then asked the reporters.

"No offensive on their part," said Frank Milbright, the *Daily Tribune* man, "but we attacked them. Yesterday, according to a Reuter's news dispatch, one of the 10-Balls hovering over a military establishment on the outskirts of Stalingrad was fired on by an atomic H-weapon. The missile never touched the 10-Ball machine proper. It ricocheted about 100 feet from it and exploded: its huge fireball was deflected *downward* as if an unseen giant force had slapped it down. In the process, the military establishment was wiped out with the loss of 795 workers, according to the Russians. The whole area was evacuated on account of the massive radioactivity contamination.

"On or about the same time, a similar attack occurred near a Federal atomic plant near Primpet, Colorado. A 10-Ball was hovering near the big plant for over an hour, when the local Nike-55 Commandant ordered the brigade to fire. Six of the recently installed Nike-55's, emplaced in a three-mile ring around the plant, went off simultaneously. The nonatomic missiles coming from all directions exploded some hundred feet from the 10-Ball, as if they had hit an invisible wall. The shell debris then scattered harmlessly over the countryside."

"This was to be expected," observed the professor. "We probably have no effective weapon on earth to attack the invaders successfully. It's like an anthill trying to attack humanity. The 10-Balls are most likely surrounded by a very powerful energy field, similar to the force that keeps electrons in place within the atom. We'd better save our ammunition—it's completely useless against these super-intelligent creatures which are most probably a million years ahead of us."

"But," another reporter wanted to know, "how do the machines communicate with each other? They *must* have a leader or commander. And if so, why can't we intercept their signals?"

"We can't answer that," replied Dubois. "We still are

C782972

woefully ignorant of countless things that have gone on for millions of years right here on earth. Take, for instance, the ants, the termites and many other insects. They communicate with each other even when separated. Some species of moths do the same. If you place a certain female moth* in an airtight box and put that box in several others, then isolate it somewhere away from other moths, a male will surely find it. So far we do not know how these communications occur, nor on what principle they work. Some scientists think it is an odor effect; if that is true, I can only say that our odor-communication technique is still at a zero level. We simply do not have any instruments or other means to intercept such signals.

"Exactly so with the invaders. That they have means of communication seems obvious. It may be telepathic or perhaps they have other means. They may employ extra-long wavelengths or *inframicro* frequencies completely out of range of our present-day detecting instruments.

"I wish to advance another thought here which our scientists and electronic specialists might ponder. Has it occurred to you that nearly all the machines may be robot or 'slave,' worked by remote control? As you well know, we have a number of remote control machines on the moon now. There are 50 or 60 on the Russian moon zone and over 100 on the U.S. moon sector, all of them operated from earth by electronics via radio.

"Thus, perhaps 999 out of 1,000 10-Balls could be worked by telecontrol from a single leading machine. Going a step further, the commanding machine could be a master robot, operated itself from outer space, or wherever they come from. There would, of course, be a number of 'spare' commanding 10-Balls should anything go wrong

*Such as the species of *Polyphemus, Promethea,* etc.

with the lead-control machine. But from what I have learned so far, I doubt that they need replacements. They are too far ahead for that."

"Another question, Professor, please," said Prentice Farragut of the Washington, D.C. *Herald*. "In your opinion, from what you have observed so far, are the invaders here to attack us, exploit us, carry off people, perhaps, or are they friendly?"

"I am happy that you brought that up, and I was particularly relieved when I heard that we attacked two of their machines with negative results. If we, from the earth, had invaded a problematical planet and *our* space machines had been attacked and fired upon, what would *we* have done? Under the rules of warfare, we would have retaliated instantly, and probably would have sacked the nearest town as an object lesson, wouldn't we?

"What did the alien invaders do when *we* attacked *them* with our best and most powerful weapons? *They ignored us!* To me this seems a good omen, at least at the moment. It begins to look as though this is a scientific research expedition. As our foremost scientists have told us for decades, it is the height of absurdity to believe that the earth is the only life-carrying planet. There must be millions of such planets in our own comparatively small universe. Given similar conditions as our own earth experienced during its nearly ten billion years of history, life would surely appear on some other planet.

"But evolution may vary widely on other worlds. Millions of grotesque species appeared on earth until man—a late-comer—finally evolved. There may even have been reasoning, intelligent species millions of years ago on earth, only to vanish for unknown reasons, like the dinosaurs.

"A similar parallel evolution must have occurred on

countless other worlds. What forms such intelligent species have taken is impossible to know. They may be mammal, bird, amphibian, insect or an unknown and quite unimaginable species. They may be huge or diminutive—nature is so full of surprises that the most grotesque creature may become dominant, as so often occurred in the past on earth.

"Just as humans are certain to explore other worlds in the future, so it was inevitable that sooner or later a race particularly far advanced in intelligence was bound to discover us and investigate the earth's dominant creatures.

"As for exploiting us, this is a difficult question. It would seem certain that almost anything that is found on earth can be found elsewhere in the Universe. That is particularly true of minerals. Spectrum analysis has shown us that almost every star is composed of the same substances that abound here on earth. Why would a far-advanced race want to traverse hostile space for trillions of miles to mine gold or uranium, when it can be found at home? I admit that certain minerals might be difficult to get at on another world, but it would seem absurd for such a super-intelligence, as we have to deal with here, to roam all over the Universe to get it. A supermind race that can build advanced machines such as are now visiting us surely can extract deeply hidden minerals from their own world—if it exists there—without difficulty.

"I admit that there might be worlds short of water—some of our own planets and our own moon have none. But how would one transport water over great distances in space? Frankly, I do not know.

"Would the invaders carry off people or certain animal species? That is an entirely different speculation. Here we have to do with an unknown type of life and their reasoning is not so obvious. So let us put ourselves in the place of a scientist for the moment. Why does an entomologist chase butterflies? He studies them and wants to know everything about them. He breeds them while they are still in the caterpillar stage. He pays attention particularly to rare types and will go to any lengths and labor to possess them.

"These earth invaders may be similarly motivated. It is logical to assume that the invading intelligence has probably never seen the like of man. Hence I would not be surprised if they were to carry off people wholesale. Indeed, it seems they made a good start with my wife and me! What puzzles us is why we were only kept—unconscious—for twenty-four hours!" Then with a wry smile, "Maybe we were poor specimens for them. Would the stolen humans be kept permanently? How can we know?" He continued:

"You understand that these can only be random opinions. It has also occurred to me that this 10-Ball fleet may be only an advance scouting force. We should not discount the possibility that another and totally different one may make an appearance later—a fleet for an entirely different purpose, which we cannot even imagine at present."

"But what can possibly be the purpose of the kind of sex research you described?" another reporter wanted to know.

"Life is sex—sex is life," was the answer. "The two are inseparable. I am convinced that our super-intelligence is a totally different species from us, and inasmuch as we appear to be intelligent to them, it is a foregone conclusion that they will study us intensely—as would we if the case were reversed.

"The human is a biological distillate that has been in an uninterrupted breeding process for hundreds of millions of years. This the invaders know. What gave us a reasoning intelligence so far superior to other earth species, to make us the dominant race? We do not know. I am positive, however, that our alien intruders will want to solve that problem. To do so they must study the whole race continuously. They must learn how we live, how we mate, how we breed, the period of gestation, birth processes and thousands of other details, many of which may be new to them and which they probably can make good use of in their own future. The higher the intellect, the more its desire to learn.

"Incidentally, while we were investigated sexologically by the invaders, the idea crossed our minds several times that, outside of the zero gravity, our experience did not differ too much from our own *sexanatoria,* now dotting the world."

"A further question, Professor," a woman newsreporter said. "Would you consider it within the realm of possibility that the alien entities could mate and breed with humans?"

"Completely impossible, as to the latter," Dubois replied. "No doubt humans have mated with the great apes countless times in the course of our long human history, but although they are our cousins, genetically speaking, there has never been an authenticated case of offspring between these races. I don't believe that there could be any children if a male human were to mate with an extra-terrestrial human-like female, or vice versa. In my own opinion, it is most doubtful that there exists anything exactly human-like outside of this planet. I would be surprised to find even a great apelike creature on another world."

"Professor," said Salzbrecht, "in our latest edition today there are a number of dispatches from all over the world, relating to cases similar to your own. In every instance, a 10-Ball machine descended over a house or dwelling place and subjected the people to a variety of enforced sex performances. In most cases the subjects seemed to be prominent, or at least active in science. What is your interpretation of that?"

"The information does not surprise me in the least. Do not forget that we are dealing with an extraordinarily high degree of intellect, far beyond anything that has ever occurred on earth. Accordingly, it was inevitable that they must have received our radio and television signals for a long time—maybe for many years. They probably recorded and translated them into their own language. Because prominent people the world over are usually mentioned by name on radio and television, the superminds stored all such information. This, again, is just one of the many possible assumptions—there may be dozens of other explanations.

"This leaves open the interesting question: How were the houses of the victims and their exact addresses learned? Once more I must impress you with the fact that we are not dealing with humans, but with superminds. Such a problem to them is, I am positive, child's play. The chances are overwhelming that we were carefully watched from a great height, perhaps several hundred miles up, for weeks or more before the actual invasion began. Minds that can build machines such as theirs must also have far-advanced instrumentation. Their *electronoptical telescopes* must be incredibly efficient. It would not surprise me to learn that they can read fine newsprint through thick walls a thousand miles distant. Don't our crude television sets, with no aerial, receive good programs through thick walls seventy-five miles away?

"It should be no trick for them to read a closed telephone directory from two hundred miles up, right through a building. It's all in the correct focusing and transmitting of energy. Again I must observe that they may use entirely different means which we in our ignorance can't even imagine.

"Why do they pick out persons who are prominent or active in science? I think I know the answer to that. When a researcher wishes to study bees, he takes great precautions not to disturb them. He knows his time will be wasted if he sticks his gloved hand into the hive. He makes his preparations with infinite care and planning. Wherever he can, he uses instruments for more effective observation. The bees never know they are being studied.

"The invading entities probably use the same reasoning. By selecting scientists and prominent people they feel that their actions will be better and more quickly understood. Thus their own research will be far more successful than if they had to deal with panicky hordes. The superminds calculate correctly that scientists particularly are apt to quiet the population once they are assured that the invasion is 'friendly.'

"And now, ladies and gentlemen, you must excuse us. We have had a difficult time, as you must realize. There is a tremendous amount of work ahead for us scientists and we must get organized rapidly, if we are to do any good in these critical times."

ECTOGENIC

CHILDREN

The Planet Invasion of June 24, 1996, was unparalleled in the world's history. Never before had the entire earth been invaded simultaneously on all its continents by an invincible alien force. Never before were all the big cities of every country threatened by a silent entity whose origin in space was unknown and which did not communicate with the earth's inhabitants nor declare the purpose of the invasion.

Within two hours after the invasion began, the heads of the world's major governments had been in frantic telephone communication to formulate a modus vivendi to meet the emergency. It was agreed by all that:

1. For twenty-four hours there would not be an overt act against the "Unknown."

2. President Hector Farragut of the U.S. was to be elected temporary chairman of the hastily formed *Invasion Intelligence*. (He was chosen chiefly because he was originally a physicist from Caltech.)

3. All the heads of the nations would confer daily at 12:00 noon with Farragut at the White House.

4. The population everywhere was to be informed by *cosmivoice* one hour after the close of the conference to remain quiet.

Soon thereafter, to allay panic and riots, all governments wisely began soothing their populations by publicizing by *cosmitronics,* then radio, television and the printed word that the invasion was a strictly scientific one for research purposes. The people were told not to resist when they came under the scrutiny of the weird floating research "laboratories." This advice proved strictly academic in the days to come, as no one was ever able to resist the will of the invader, no matter what schemes were tried to circumvent the alien force.

The invasion had come so suddenly that before orders could be given to the military "not to commit an overt act," Russia as well as the U.S. had fired on two overhead 10-Balls, with the results already chronicled. Thereafter, for quite a while, the military forces of the world obeyed the order of nonaggression.

Within five hours of the invasion, the cosmivoice boomed in every home within reach of a government C.V. (cosmivoice) transmitter. It was a short announcement designed mainly to quiet the population everywhere.

(The cosmivoice, invented by Vitello Camarro in 1978, uses micro-micro cosmic waves. When these waves hit a house, an automobile or *airobile* overhead, the walls, windows or the structure itself gives forth loud sound, as if a tremendous loudspeaker were trained on it. The action of the cosmic waves, however, differs from older methods in that they set up *molecular* vibrations in the walls, whether they are of stone, glass or metal. These vibrations are then resolved into audible sound. Thus no one in any building or conveyance can escape the all-pervading voice. The cosmivoice is used only in emergency—for defense, war and disaster purposes. It has supplanted all air-raid alarms.)

Less than a week after the invasion, Professor Duke Dubois had organized a team of leading U.S. scientists to gather all pertinent facts pertaining to the invaders. As president of the ten-year-old *International Science Foundation,* which had member-scientists all over the globe, he also immediately organized a constantly increasing flow of dispatches and reports which the Foundation's scientists gathered personally from all those persons who had been seized and temporarily detained in their homes by a 10-Ball machine.

It very quickly became clear that the aim of the invader was purely research, at least thus far. The usual pattern was similar to what Professor Dubois and his wife had experienced. It appeared that the Unknown was making an exhaustive survey of the human sexual mores, reproduction, gestation, birth processes and other sexological behavior. Evidently the invader was minutely examining and "processing" all races on all the continents, just as a top ant entomologist, while engaged in writing an outstanding textbook, would personally examine specimens of live ants from every continent of the world.

In one of Dubois' symposiums with a large staff of scientists and technicians, the question of the propulsion and mode of operation of the now-famed 10-Balls came under full discussion. The consensus, later released to the press—shorn of much of its technicality—ran somewhat as follows:

Apparently the propelling force was intimately linked with the nine rotating spheres. The large top sphere, some 75 feet in diameter, with its somewhat flattened bottom, was the center of operations and, perhaps, the power plant. The nine smaller balls, each about 40 feet in diameter, rotated clockwise, as seen from below. There was no visible connection between any of the ten spheres. What held them all together? Obviously a force similar to that which holds electrons in their orbits as they rotate about the nucleus of an atom. That force, scientists are agreed, is perhaps the most powerful in the universe, next to gravitation.

It seems certain that the Unknown Entity, millions of years ahead of our civilization, had solved the riddle of the atom as well as of gravitation, and perhaps of other forces of which we are not even aware.

From the bottom of the large top sphere to well below the bottom tier of the six lower rotating spheres there extends a huge, hazy, purple tube. This tube normally is between 150 and 200 feet long. It can, however, be lengthened at will by its "operator." The tube appears to be not solid but highly flexible. It probably rotates on its axis, but on that point opinions are divided. It may be a specially dense gas, or it may be composed of myriads of heavy particles held together and in place by some unknown force. The open end of the tube is large enough to envelop a four-storey house.

Investigators have never been able to come closer to it than about ten feet. The tube is not only charged with a peculiar form of electrical high-ampere current, but is surrounded on the *outside* with a tremendous force-field, which also surrounds all the balls. The force of this field is so tremendous that even a A-bomb can be deflected without harm to the machine, as was noted on the first day of the invasion.

The majority opinion of those scientists who had an opportunity during the invasion to investigate the machines intensely from the ground with many instrumentalities— such as high-speed photography, magnetoelectric, spectrum analytical, radar, cosmotronical, gravitoelectronic and many others—was that *the 10-Ball machines are propelled and steered by an electromagnetical-gravitational force or power.*

This was best demonstrated by the fact that when a machine hovered about 300 feet directly over a house or dwelling, the house and everything in it acquired zero gravity. That was also the direct cause of the tornado-like wind. As all the air in the house became weightless, it rushed out explosively. At the same time, the heavy outside air pushed into the quasi-vacuum of the dwelling.

When the purple tube completely enveloped the house, the wind always stopped, since no outside air could flow past or through the walls of the tube. Whatever air there was in the house stayed in it.

But directly under the machine, zero gravity remained; hence everything in the house was weightless. If you blew hard against a book or a lamp resting on a table, either object would sail off the table and perhaps hit against the wall and stay suspended there.

The electromagnetic effects of the tremendous force-field of the 10-Balls also raise havoc with the communications systems in a house once the hollow tube has descended over it. Hence phones, radios, television, even the cosmivoice are always interrupted and out of order.

When the 10-Ball lifted up slowly at the end of its mission, normal gravity in the house was gradually returned. Once the machine attained an altitude of over 500 feet, the gravitational effect directly under it became dissipated. Our earth acts in a similar manner—the higher you get away from it, the less the attraction. Thus, if you weigh 150 pounds at sea level, your weight is only 96 pounds 1,000 miles up.

* * *

A few days after the invasion, Duke and Donny were finishing a rather silent dinner. This was unusual, as Duke customarily was quite animated and rarely came home without a good story, anecdote or one of his own humorous concoctions, for which he was famous. While sipping her demitasse of *café turque,* Donny broke the silence.

"What have the 10-Ball gremlins been up to today? You look as if you were behind the 10-Balls yourself!"

Smiling faintly, Duke reached over and took Donny's hand and said, "Come!"

They walked silently to the bedroom, to the obvious puzzlement of Donny. His manner was inexplicably strange and there was an unusual expression in his eyes. Nor was this their usual hour for lovemaking.

He touched a button on the wall which closed all the drapes. He then closed the door.

"Undress, please," he said softly.

"Completely?" she half-protested, wide-eyed.

"Yes, dear, completely."

"But, Duke," she exclaimed incredulously, "aren't you undressing, too?"

"No—not yet, dear, later." This in a curiously strained voice.

She disrobed quickly, and soon stood in the nude with a puzzled look on her face.

Duke turned on the crystal ceiling chandelier and placed Donny in its full glare. From his pocket he drew forth his library high-power magnifying glass and proceeded to examine her minutely, going over every part of her milk-white body.

He finished, while shaking his head, and, with a sigh, said in a flat voice:

"Darling, I am pained to report that you are going to become a mother! You had better dress again."

Donny had stifled a cry, her right hand over her breast, as she sank on the bed. Duke tenderly put his arm around her while she cried softly.

"No, no," she sobbed. "They couldn't, the inhuman beasts—tell me it isn't so!" She had, with woman's intuition, divined immediately that there was something fiendish behind all this and that the Unknowns were at the bottom of it.

"Unfortunately, dear, it is all too true—we are now breeding for the invasion entity," was his sad, almost apologetic answer.

"But how did I get pregnant?"

"I didn't say you were pregnant—only that you are going to be a mother," was Duke's reply.

"As I probably will be the father, I am even more pained to tell you that we probably will never see our child—*and you are not going to give birth to him or her!*"

Donny was too shocked and bewildered to talk.

Duke continued. "You see, Donny, we are not dealing with humans—once and for all you must adjust your thinking. Try to imagine the earth as it might be a million years hence, if you can. Everything has changed here *now*. There are new laws, new values, new customs, and for a while we must live with them, difficult as it is bound to be.

"To start at the beginning. You remember that on the day of the invasion, we lost a full day? Well, it seems this is the present pattern with everyone who has been forced to have intercourse by our new master. On the basis of reports from over two hundred scientists, who examined the subjects minutely after their ordeal, the puzzle-picture has started to come into focus.

"Every individual 'processed' by the invaders showed curious punctures—we call them 'Sex Punctures.' On the females there usually are several punctures on the low abdomen above one or both ovaries, in the region where the fallopian tubes are located.

"On the males, the punctures are in the upper part of the scrotum, where the epididymis is found. In the male, this is the only site of the puncture. In the female, there may be others, on the inside of the arm or on the leg. Look!"

With that, Duke handed Donny the magnifying glass. There were two curious reddish marks, smaller than a pin head, one to the left, one to the right of her abdomen. There was also a somewhat larger mark on the inside of the arm fold.

"But what does this all signify?" Donny wanted to know.

"I think we have the answer," Duke proceeded. "By some means we have not perfected today, but which have been forecast since the forties, the superminds have long abandoned our crude X rays and now probably use *opaquepenetrators*. If you have a sufficiently strong light source, say 10-20 million candlepower, and turn it on your hand, you should be able to see through it, not only see all bones, but every muscle, every blood vessel, every nerve. To do so, the outline of the hand must be tightly blocked so that no light shines in your eyes while you examine the hand behind. The light must also be focused exactly on the internal spot you wish to see. Furthermore, you must filter out the heat rays, otherwise the hand will be burned.

"Our superbrains were looking for human sex cells. By means of the opaquepenetrator, or similar means, they transilluminated us from the rear. In the darkroom, it was

then possible to see the inside of your fallopian tubes, and by means of a special magnifier locate one of your ovulated ova, or eggs, as it wandered down into the womb. The female human egg is smaller than the period after a printed word, thus it is extremely difficult to see it, but with suitable magnification it can be spotted and extracted with a special hollow needle and syringe. As a woman ovulates only once a month, there must have been an egg in your fallopian tube, otherwise they would not have punctured your abdomen.

"The male sperm is much easier to get at, and as there are many thousands in a very small area, it is simple to syringe them out from the epididymis.

"There only remains the comparatively simple task of fertilizing the ovum with the sperm and the new child is conceived and on the way.

"We also think we've found the reason why we, as well as all the other subjects who were captured, were forced to have such long and repeated intercourse.

"Obviously, it would be much simpler for the superbrain technicians if they could extract an ovum that was already fertilized. Then they would not have to do the fertilizing of the ovum themselves in the laboratory.

"Hence they forced us into repeated copulation so as to be reasonably sure that—if there was an egg—fecundation had taken place naturally when they finally extracted the ovum while we were unconscious.

"But not all couples are fertile—for instance, we are not. There is also the matter of contraception. A woman may wear a diaphragm or use other means. The male may use a sheath. For that reason, to be on the safe side, while the laboratory technicians have the couple in captivity and at their mercy, they will also extract the male's sperm—as they did with me and with nearly all the other males."

"But who and what will feed the fetus?" Donny asked, wide-eyed.

"You will!" said Duke, "believe it or not, albeit in absentia."

"How on earth can that be possible?"

"Remember the puncture inside your arm? Well, this had us puzzled for a while, but suddenly I remembered an old monograph from the year 1945, and the jigsaw puzzle picture was completed.

"A generous amount of blood was taken from your arm, to 'type' your blood. After typing, a serum was prepared and that will feed the embryo and, later, the fetus as it grows. It will be your blood, and I am reasonably certain it is your ovum and my sperm. Hence *we* will be the parents."

"But how can one be certain that my ovum will be fertilized by your sperm? You know we tried to have children for years and couldn't."

"Even our own backward geneticists and sexological scientists have made some headway in that direction. In 10,000 years, not to speak of a million, practually every couple desirous of children will have them. So far we know of certain things necessary for fertilization. One of them is the chemical *hyaluronidase*. If the male sperm is deficient in it, there will be no fertilization. We can be certain that our superminds will use special additives when they breed humans—they will have no failures, I am positive of that."

Donny was silent, lost in deep thought after hearing the remarkable forecast.

"But, Duke," she breathed plaintively, "what will happen to our child and to all the other human children, brought up without the guidance of a human mother?"

"We don't know—all is conjecture—but my own guess is that for the first few years, they'll have a warm human-like soft, plastic robot mother. It probably will even have human-like breasts that will feed the child with synthetic milk. *We know this for certain because in a number of the captured cases there were young mothers, all of whom were breast-feeding their infants.* In these particular cases, there were no forced sex exhibitions. Instead, an advanced hypnotic technique was used for only a few hours. During that time, while the subjects were in a trance, live mother's milk was probably aspirated to be synthetized by the superminds.

"Finally, no one can be certain *when* the fertilizing process will be used. For over a generation, on earth, sperm has been stored under high refrigeration, often for many years. Ova have been similarly stored for the past decade. Children have actually been born for a long time now, many years after the husband had died, as a result of insemination of the wife with the long deceased husband's sperm.

"We shall therefore probably never know if our child will be born in nine months, a decade, or a century from now. We should keep this in mind before we become too emotional on this painful subject."

INVASION

JITTERS

After the first few weeks of the invasion, the heads of The Big-5 nations met in solemn session in Washington's White House. President Hector Farragut of the U.S. had called the extraordinary meeting to discuss future action on *The Xeno from Space,** as the invader was now generally referred to.

Present were the representatives of the nations who had stockpiles of atomic A- and H-bombs and who had just started on the manufacture of the even more devastating Cosmic X-Bomb, whose instant-deadly radiation far exceeded the killing power of the largest H-bombs. The great difference in the new bomb was that it caused no physical damage to either property or even people, but it could instantly kill millions of persons in a large city by

---

*Xeno, from the Greek; strange, foreign, extraneous, as in xenophobia. After the invasion there were continuous outbreaks of xenophobia.

radiation alone.

The list comprised President Hector Farragut of the U.S.; Premier Malcolm Breckenridge of Great Britain; Premier Georgi Popoff of the U.S.S.R.; President Aristide Desvalieres of France; and Premier Kamakura Tokugawa of Japan. The meeting was completely secret and the actual proceedings did not become known until much later. The gist of the talks ran as follows:

The nations recognized immediately that the world had met a new and superior force as well as a hyper-intelligence whose extent could not even be encompassed.

The consensus was that the invader should not be challenged or molested for the present, as long as his intent remained "peaceful." Indeed, inasmuch as even H-bombs were completely ignored by him, what challenge could there be so far to confront the Xeno from Space?

All those present agreed to set up at once a World Alliance of Five to deal jointly with the invader and to set the future policy on a worldwide basis. While there was little love lost between some of the governments, and while a refined type of cold war had persisted between much of the East and West, every head of state knew full well that in a forest fire lions do not attack other lions, or gazelles. Now that a potentially overwhelming new foe had appeared, humanity for once had to stand together in a united peace front. Major and even "little" wars were unthinkable now, and one of the first documents of the meeting was a treaty signed by all heads of the assembled nations. The signatories agreed that "for the duration, and until one year after the invasion" no overt action would be taken by any member nation against any other nation, and that in the unlikely event that non-signatory nations attacked the World Alliance of Five, the United Nations would be called upon to arbitrate a peaceful settlement.

The second urgent proposal on the agenda was that all member nations should pledge themselves to explore, through their scientists and technicians, every possible means of discovering an "Achilles heel" of the 10-Balls. All research of the whole Alliance was to be centered immediately upon this problem and every member state was to be informed of such progress. The only dissenter during this debate was Russia's shrewd Premier Georgi Popoff, who was also a champion chessplayer.

"Gentlemen," he began in his fluid Oxford English, "I must call your attention to a fact which perhaps you have overlooked. Our own intelligence reports point to the unmistakable possibility that the White House at this very moment is certain to be under complete surveillance by our uninvited 'guests.' From what your own scientists have told you, the invading entity has means to see and hear through multiple walls without any difficulty. We are today nothing but goldfish in a glass bowl—everything we do, every sound we utter, every note we write, is, I am positive, recorded in one of the 10-Balls. Speaking for my country, I, for one, will do nothing to incur the wrath or displeasure of our—so far—very peaceful research entity."

At this point, Malcolm Breckenridge, British Premier, did an unusual thing. He sat down, then pointedly winked at each member. Everyone assembled immediately understood the maneuver as a gesture for more secrecy. and, for the next ten minutes the debate was along minor "non-political" issues.

Later, Breckenridge strolled over to each of his four confrères and carefully whispered an identical message into his ear.

"Adjourn. Await my messenger with your chief scientist tonight at 7:00 P.M."

Breckenridge's messengers later in the day delivered to

each member nation a heavy block of metal weighing 55 pounds. There was also a very heavy helmet. The attaché who had delivered the "message" personally to President Farragut whispered a few words into the ear of Ulysses Cosimer, the President's Science Coordinator, who had been summoned earlier.

Cosimer put on the heavy cumbersome helmet, pressed a button on the hexagon object that immediately illuminated a small circle on the top of the cube. He glued his eye to the lighted circle, which proved to be a powerful lens. Below he saw an engraved plate which read:

"This cube is made of an alloy of lead and *Russium* (the 112th element). The combination is not radioactive. All known radiations, including cosmic, cannot penetrate this alloy if walls are over 2″ thick. Helmet is of same material. Suggest each member of the Alliance construct an alloy underground meeting room accommodating 12 persons. Propose next meeting in Paris 30 days hence.

"Memorize message—do not copy."

After a few minutes, Cosimer handed the helmet to the President, who donned it and for some minutes studied the strange message. He and Cosimer then held a whispered conference and, in turn, the President whispered his acceptance to Breckenridge's attaché.

Similar scenes were enacted at the embassies of the other Alliance members, all agreeing to accept the plan and to meet in Paris in 30 days.

Curiously enough, Cosimer on the same morning had read a report on the identical subject by his own science staff. It was entitled "All Frequency Barrier." The material was similar to lead and Russium 112. It stopped all known radiation waves and rays by total absorption. It did not *reflect* waves which could be returned to the sender, like radar, and then amplified. Breckenridge's idea for total security against the advanced invader appeared flawless to all scientists consulted later in man-to-man whispered conferences.

The first AFBE Secret Room in the hemisphere was constructed in Washington in less than ten days. It became known as an AFBE (from *A*ll *F*requency *B*arrier *E*nclosure) and nowadays dots the world's radiation laboratories. Such rooms were of course prime security equipment for all "political" talks during the invasion.

Every power instantly recognized that sooner or later the invader would not be the sole possessor of *"infinite sight and sound amplification,"* as the scientists called it. Indeed, by 1996 considerable progress had been made in this direction by all nations. The U.S. Armed Forces since 1990 had a field sound amplifier which worked up to twenty miles. By training their *Sound Multiplier* on a house twenty miles distant, they could record a conversation with perfect clarity despite thick walls. This was their *modulated audioradar* beam, perfected after it had become possible to filter all extraneous and unwanted sounds from the beam.

Reading telephone-book type over great distances, as scientists felt the invader could do, proved more troublesome, but it was predicted that the twenty-first century would almost certainly solve that problem.

In the meanwhile, every cabinet meeting of all great powers was held in an AFBE. So were those of the military staffs, as fast as the secret rooms could be built. The reasoning went somewhat like this:

It was not only the invader who had to be watched, but the intelligence departments of every one of the big nations had become suspect. How could the Pentagon in Washington, for instance, be certain that the various embassies would not soon spy on the U.S. secret conferences? With the technical refinements now being perfected, it would soon be impossible for friend or foe alike to detect such spying methods even with the best instrumentation.

Hence, the frantic building of AFBE's at all strategic points. As an AFBE could never have windows, practically all such totally secret rooms were placed underground. Walls, ceilings, floors and doors all had to be constructed of the lead-russium (or similar) alloy. For further security, there were no phones—talks could be detected by "distant-tapping" of the wires. Light was provided by standard, no outside wire atomelectronics. Fresh air was brought in through a complex lead-russium filter system, first through water traps and then filtered again. All machinery was self-contained atomelectronic power. There were no wires connecting an AFBE.

Secret documents were now carried by armed messengers in closed cubes of radiation-proof material to other AFBE's. In this fashion, practically all spying in this sphere was stopped.

At the state dinner given by President Farragut for the four visiting Premiers before their departure, there were a few last whispered conversations. Curiously enough, Popoff voiced his great pleasure at the idea of the new secret rooms and, as he put it cryptically, "We can all relax now without fear of spies or other unpleasantness."

Popoff's enthusiastic endorsement of the secret-proof rooms was by no means a sincere one. His intelligence personnel must have known for some time that radiation-proof materials were "in the air," as is frequently the case of simultaneous discoveries and inventions in various parts of the world.

As the excellent chessplayer that he was, he wanted to be a few moves ahead of the pack, hence his dissent at the White House with the proposal to locate the weak spot of

the Xenos—if there was one. As became known later by
our own intelligence, Popoff had actually constructed an
AFBE weeks before he came to the White House for the
World Alliance of Five session! This was a typical Popoff
maneuver. Indeed, his own scientists had been given all-out
priority orders to detect a weakness or flaw in the
armament of the invader and to bring down a 10-Ball at all
costs, short of direct attack. Whatever secrets were to be
wrested from the invader would then be the U.S.S.R.'s, for
the control of the world. He did not intend to share them
with the other nations.

But he had other reasons, too. Good ones—and highly
personal ones. And they were not pleasant, either!

For months, what later became known euphoniously as
"Popoff's Ordeal" was supposed to have been a well-
guarded secret. But somehow the piquant story was quickly
whispered around in the high circles of Moscow. It never
reached the controlled press, for obvious reasons. The West
did not hear of it until much later.

It seems that Popoff, just turned sixty-three, was at
home one night in his dacha, a beautiful villa fifteen miles
from Moscow. In his youth, Popoff had married Olga, a
much older woman. They had no children.

But it was also known that for some years he had been
seriously involved with a much younger and very beautiful
ex-ballerina. Because of an accident to her foot she could
no longer appear on the stage. Popoff, as was well known
to the higher echelons of the hierarchy, spent five out of
seven nights with his *dulcinea,* Anushka Petrova, at her
modest but chic dacha, not far from his own home.

Madame Popoff, of course, was well aware of this
arrangement, but, like many other high-placed Russian
wives in similar positions, she seemed not to care.
Moreover, she was advanced in years, and, as wife of the

Premier, her high station, plus security, made up for her husband's regular Don Juaneries.

Had she not said to a confidante: "Georgi must have adventure—it keeps him young and on his mettle. Besides, he *always* comes back to me."

But, as the French say: *Revenons à nos moutons!*—back to our story.

Three days after the historic invasion, Popoff *had* come back home to his wife, after a hard day's work at the Kremlin. The night was hot, and as often happened, the Premier and his wife slept in the nude under their heavy linen sheets.

Without warning, a 10-Ball descended over Popoff's dacha and within seconds the house-tornado had set in. After the purple tube had settled over the villa and the house-storm had died down, the heavy aphrodisiac air-current drifted in rapidly and the Popoffs were enveloped in it. As usual, it permeated the entire house. They were already experiencing zero gravity, too.

Georgi Popoff could not resist the silent but imperious command of the invader any better than anyone else, and soon, to the utter amazement of Madame Popoff, the couple found themselves transported into a never-before-experienced Eden of marital delights.

They were sound asleep next morning when the strange tinkling of broken bric-a-brac awoke them, and they watched in amazement as the pieces were joined together magically by the superminds.

Just as they were dressing, the purple tube lifted. Their two elderly servants burst in after repeatedly knocking at the bedroom door, thoroughly befuddled and crossing themselves in fright. Living in the same house, they had of course been subject to similar sex experiences. They tremulously inquired as to the health of their masters.

They were immediately told that, if they valued their lives, not a word of their experiences must go out to anyone.

By this time the security police had arrived and they, too, were cautioned by Popoff that for "security's sake" nothing of Popoff's ordeal was to be made public under pain of severe reprisal. The police understood perfectly and soon withdrew. In Russia, where it is not safe to loiter near the Premier's home, hardly a soul was in sight. Nevertheless, the invader's descent over Popoff's dacha was known almost immediately all over the neighborhood—but for the time being, no one knew what actually had happened at the dacha—and the old servants didn't talk. Much later, naturally, the secret had leaked out, but by that time it was past history.

Popoff, of course, had to give his colleagues a full report, but they, too, at first, kept the secret.

Characteristically, Popoff made light of his "ordeal." He boasted that he, for one, was very happy that it had been his privilege to be selected by the invader for such "interesting scientific research." It would enable the Premier to understand the Xenos much better and perhaps devise means to deal with them.

Furthermore, he had always had a strong desire to experience zero gravity for more than the few minutes he had experienced it when, as a young colonel, he had been shot 400 miles up above the atmosphere, becoming a hero after his safe landing.

As to the—ah—forced marital union, there was nothing to that. He would make a full technical report to the Genetic Society in due time.

Privately, he was in a rage. He knew that his mistress must have heard about his experience, because she lived not too far away. Had the two not talked about the sexual connotations of the invasion only a day ago? As he was genuinely in love with Anushka, how could he face her? How could he explain the intimacy with his elderly wife? He was furious at the invaders and swore to avenge himself.

Even before he went back to Anushka, Popoff had to vent his true feelings to the only man he could trust, his oldtime buddy, General Dmitri Troyanovsky.

"Why," he kept moaning over and over, "couldn't they have chosen Anushka's dacha—what a feast we could have had!"

One bright facet of his ordeal—it lasted but six hours, so he was told by the security staff. Evidently, after the Xeno-technicians had ascertained that the humans in the dacha were both elderly, they shortened the research, even though they punctured the epididymis of Popoff in one spot, and the abdomen of his wife on her left side. The same was the case with the servants, a man and wife team.

It should be noted for the record that the reaction of Madame Popoff differed diametrically from that of her husband. Said she to her old confidante:

"Tatiana, you wouldn't believe it. Georgi that night—he was magnificent! Even better than on our wedding night!"

It was not long thereafter that Popoff, and later every head of all nations—who could afford the high cost—built an AFBE on his estate. These were chiefly used as sleeping quarters.

In case a 10-Ball descended over them, the invader could not get at the people. As all AFBE's were hermetically sealed off, a tornado inside was impossible. The air-conditioner filtered all incoming air through water and other neutralizing chemicals, thus no gas, aphrodisiac or otherwise, could reach those inside.

True, as long as a 10-Ball was overhead, zero-gravity *would* occur within the AFBE, if the invader hovered low.

But that, not too surprisingly, was a very desirable eventuality which most married couples fondly looked forward to!

* * *

The week of July 24, 1996, heralded the first full month of the world's historic invasion. For the teeming masses—the six billion inhabitants of the earth—it had been a month of utter confusion, frustration, upheaval and anger. The world, now over 91 percent literate, was well read and well informed, thanks to the amazing progress of communications and technology.

Newspapers electronically "printed" on *paplast** rolled off the presses simultaneously in several thousand cities all over the world, in many languages, from New York, London, Moscow and Tokyo news headquarters. The four huge newspaper centers supplied the news and advertisements via *facsimile television,* which were then automatically "matriced" in finished metal plates right on the newspaper presses. The presses then started rolling within fifteen minutes, delivering finished papers. Local news and advertisements were of course supplied on a separate sheet (or page) by the electronic printing plant.

Naturally, the paplast press had kept up with every available scrap of invasion information, no matter where its origin.

Naturally, also, the sensational paplast tabloids had a field day, every day, with lurid local disclosures about those

*Paplast (from *paper* + *plastics), a synthetic paper substitute, had been made on a large scale since 1984. Manufactured from sand (silicon), air and atomically conveyed coal, it was cheaper than paper, did not tear easily, and could be made in all colors. Newspapers were no longer printed with ink, hence never blackened the hands. Impressions were made *electrically* while the paplast sheet was moist. Paplast contained chemicals which, when treated electrically, created the printing of any color desired. It "set" permanently, never discolored.

persons who unhappily had been "kidnaped" for one or more days. An entirely new nomenclature sprang up, to no one's surprise, to fit the extraordinary situation into which the world was plunged so suddenly.

Such terms as "sexnaping," "sexbandits," "sexperimenters," "sexplorers," "sexmechanics" were only a few. The serene anonymity of the invaders, who gave never a hint of their nature or origin, became the most irritating and exasperating feature of the invasion. They were quickly dubbed "Space Fiends," "Spacebrains," "Telebrains," "Spacegimmickers," "Spaceaces" and hundreds of other names.

Beneath it all, despite the sardonic humor of the masses, who continued to treat the *sex-invasion*—a term quickly introduced—lightheartedly, there was a constant gnawing worry and fear of the Xenos.

What were they really up to? What would they do after they finished their sex research with the humans? Would there be a second and an entirely different type of invasion? Would they make war on humanity? Would they, perhaps, carry off large slices of the earth's population?

It became known soon from the various science reports that the superminds were probably breeding humans as we breed cattle. But what was their ultimate object? Obviously, they would carry off the newly bred ectogenic humans. But where to? For what purpose? Human zoos on a far distant planet or in another time stratum?

Those were the exasperating and frustrating questions that begged for perpetual answers, which were not forthcoming.

Added to this multibillion chorus were the voices of that great elite, the fifteen thousand or so odd victims, the "processed" ones, who suddenly had been lifted to prominence, hero worship and high distinction. Practically

all of them, once they had been minutely grilled by scores
of scientists and submitted to their most painstaking
questionnaires, were now prime targets of the paplast press,
the magazines, the radio and television.

They were considered the front-line soldiers of the
invasion and were treated accordingly by the population.
As all of them had been more or less prominent
before—*the Xenos chose only highly placed people as their
victims*—their opinions, and pronouncements were highly
regarded and listened to with respect. This was particularly
true of editorial writers who had the job of molding public
opinion in those frenetic days.

Loudest were the outraged voices from the leaders of the
hundreds of various religions of the earth. There was not a
religion that condoned the invader's ruthless liberties with
the sanctity of the individual's body. The churches
thundered their wrath in an ever-mounting denunciation in
the daily press, even though they knew that their vociferous
protests were of no avail. Choleric letters "To the Editor"
echoed editorials and articles on the subject of "enforced
sex enslavement of our prominent people."

There were many excellent editorials on the subject of
"the present lamentable and shameful debasement of
man," yet there were, curiously enough, dissenters. We
quote only one of these, a lone wolf's voice, in an editorial
which, nevertheless, was widely reprinted as a sign of the
times. It appeared in the highly respected Nairobi (Kenya)
Africa Times. Here is the gist:

EROTIC SOUR GRAPES?

For many weeks on end, we have now followed the
extraordinary parade of articles and editorials in the
international press spewing forth sulfurous flames of
indignation at the sex research of our otherwise peaceful

invaders. So far, at least—and let us be profoundly grateful for that—there has been no war, no recent casualties, no mayhem, no widespread destruction. Certainly we are the last to submit that we were pleased with the invasion and that we approve of it. Nonetheless, where is there a thinking person who doesn't tremble at the thought of how infinitely worse an *enemy* invasion could be, with millions of dead strewing the earth.

From the number of frank talks we have had with frank and truthful souls—some of them high-placed folk—we believe we detect an undercurrent of sentiment which is not at all homogeneous with that of the protesting masses.

Is it possible that envy taints the opinion of so many? There are—and we feel that their names are legion—those adventurous souls who are constantly hoping against hope that *they* will be selected as the ones to be "exploited shamefully" as the only too willing victims of the Xenos, so they, too, might explore the fabled sexual delights of zero gravity. They, too, would like nothing better than to strut in front of the populace, be acclaimed heroes and become "prominents"—V.I.P.'s, as our American cousins call them.

Yes, we fear, frustration and jealousy can warp one's opinion badly.

5

PORTENTOUS

REVELATIONS

During the second month of the invasion by the *Xeno from Space,* Duke Dubois, as president of the International Science Foundation, directed his staff to prepare a comprehensive report on the varifold activities of the invader. Much had been learned during the first month of the occupation, and new information came to light continuously. The invader, it seemed, was much more complex than was realized at first. It became apparent, too, that his mission on earth was to be quite extensive and that it had been planned very methodically. Many scientists predicted the possibility of many astonishing denouements that might shake the world profoundly.

We shall attempt here to list only a few of the highlights of the report.

1. The questions which puzzled scientists and psychologists as well as laymen were: How does the invader proceed in making and keeping his captives unconscious for days? How does he blot out memories of things he does not wish them to remember?

The answers: A recent breakthrough to be released simultaneously with this report sheds much light on these questions. Professor Wolfgang Erhofen, of the Yale Psychophysics Department, reported that in questioning several hundred persons kidnaped by the invader, it was discovered that two of the victims, who had been in auto accidents, were wearing the usual steel neckbrace collars to immobilize broken necks or spines.

It had already been ascertained that, during the deep sleep following the forced intercourse proceedings, all subjects were placed, by *telehypnosis,* into a further and much deeper sleep, from which they did not awake until commanded by the invader-technician.

This was proved by the fact that several persons in an adjoining house were *partly* affected by telehypnosis. That also proved that telehypnosis went *beyond* the purple tube in certain cases.

Scientists are not certain that the method used is truly hypnotic—there may be other means used by the superbrains which we do not know.

In any event, the two subjects who wore the steel collars did not fall into a paralyzing sleep as did all other persons. They reported that they were semi-conscious part of the time. One—Frank Alzette, a Chicago electronics inventor of note—remembered that he and his wife were "ordered" to walk near the purple tube's interior, where he—not his wife, who was in a trance—felt an indescribable tingling inside his body. Then they were wafted by some non-material (not solid, he said) means—probably in zero gravity—upward into an eerie green phosphorescence. They had been totally nude since intercourse—which in zero gravity did not seem to affect his neck adversely—and he felt slightly chilly 300 feet up in the top ball, where he thought they were. He and his wife were placed side by side on an unsupported transparent slab that had many contraptions, which he glimpsed through his partly closed eyes. The slab probably was in zero gravity. Both he and his wife were secured to the slab by elastic grippers.

In the weak green light, he faintly saw an egg-shaped helmet with two enormous luminous eyes staring intently at his wife. He was not certain that what he saw *were* eyes—they could have been optical means of some sort. The egg-shaped helmet was large on top and narrow under the head, while the body of the operator was encased in a brown plastic-like material. It was smooth and shiny. The creature, as it bent down, appeared as large as, or larger than, a human. No feet or legs were glimpsed. Two assistants floating in were also totally encased. Judging from the helmets, which seemed to be of metal—the outline of the heads could not be seen through the transparent curved faceplate—the heads, if they were heads, seemed much larger than human ones.

On top of the helmet there were a number of curious articulated members, which at times moved with extraordinary motions. Some seemed to carry lenses.

The light in the circular "room" in which Alzette and his sleeping wife were was so weak that he had only a hazy impression of the walls. The nearer wall—if wall it was—had an indescribable array of phantasmic gadget-apparatus, many of which were in a nightmare-like motion.

He had a good glimpse of the one who seemed to be the chief Xeno technician. He seemed totally enclosed in a spacelike plastic-appearing suit. Alzette observed that there were four flexible, thin, armlike appendages also enclosed in the same brown plastic-like material. Each end of the arm had a round revolvable ball which carried ten highly complex metal "fingers." These fingers were actually different tools, each having a specific function. The "fingers" worked so fast it was impossible to watch their motions simultaneously. The huge eyes, which seemed to have no lids, stared fixedly on the work before them.

Alzette saw a complicated apparatus appear over his wife's abdomen, which settled down after a few motions. One of the technicians moved his head and peered into it for a few seconds. While one of his forty metal fingers moved a rod, other fingers did other things so fast Alzette could not follow their motion. It was over in seconds. Then another type of machine flowed over his wife's thigh and the technician went through a similar routine lasting about a minute. Alzette guessed later that the first machine had extracted an ovum from his wife, while the second machine siphoned off a quantity of her blood.

How the Xeno "chief" and his technicians communicated is not known. Alzette heard nothing. As the technicians were totally enclosed, the talk—if there was any—could only have been by telephone inside the helmets or other means, perhaps telepathic.

It was then Alzette's turn. A machine smaller than the one used on his wife's abdomen floated over his left groin and the "operation" took place to extract a quantity of his sperm. He remembered that he had felt practically nothing. Then he noted that a faint, pink fluorescence appeared at the top of the chief's helmet. Another stronger, dark-red beam joined it. Both light rays seemed to come from two different openings of the helmet at the base of a round prominence. The merged single ray was now focused on Alzette's wife's forehead. It stayed there a few seconds.

Then it was his turn. The instant the ray touched his forehead, everything went blank. He went into a deep sleep. He and his wife awoke two days later. The 10-Ball had gone.

He immediately noticed that his neck went strange. Carefully, he took off his heavy neckbrace.

His broken neck had been completely repaired, as if it never had been broken. What the technicians had done to accomplish this feat, no one knows at present. It should be noted here that the other man—Archibald Gatsby of Melbourne, Australia—observed very much the same things as did Alzette. Both their reports checked closely. Gatsby's broken collarbone, too, was completely healed on his return home.

It would seem that the steel braces made it possible for the two humans to remember later what they had experienced. The pink-red ray evidently was usually trained on the memory center by the invaders, and in every case except the two mentioned, the memory of what the humans had experienced *after* the red rays touched them, was completely blotted out.

Professor Wolfgang Erhofen's recent breakthrough on memory techniques seems to parallel the invader's.

Erhofen calls his new discovery *telekomen* (from the Greek: *tele* for far, *elegchos* for control, *menos* for mind), in other words, *Distant Mind Control.* He uses ultra sound, modulated with low power, soft X rays, filtered through a Russium screen, which do not harm the body. By these means he can blot out forever certain memories which adversely affect an individual. He makes the subject describe out loud the offensive incident while the rays are turned on in the region of the memory center of the brain. This wipes out that particular part of the memory, just as a magnet wipes off unwanted dictation forever from the magnetic tape of a dictation machine.

2. Why do the invaders wear airtight "space suits"? This puzzled scientists for a while, but Professor Duke Dubois gave the logical and—as far as is known—correct answer.

When the invaders process humans, they must meet them in their own surroundings. When men go down to study deep-sea fish, they must use a bathysphere to descend to the great depths. There the fish are under thousands of tons of water pressure. If you bring the fish out of their surroundings, they explode near the surface.

The Xenos evidently cannot live in either the earth's high air pressure or its atmosphere. Perhaps they normally live in very rarefied air that may not even contain nitrogen, as our planet's air does. Furthermore, there is the very important matter of germs, viruses and other organisms. Human germs or viruses may kill the invaders, *theirs* may kill humans. Hence, if they are to make contact with humans and study them, they must completely isolate themselves from earth inhabitants. Thus, they can meet humans only in their own low-pressure suits, while the latter remain in their own high-pressure, high bacteria-laden air.

After the Xenos finished their experiments with the humans, they presumably entered their own atmosphere-chamber where their space suits were left, to be disinfected and thoroughly cleaned. Then they stepped into another of their atmospheric locks, and thence returned to their own quarters.

3. The various governments were severely criticized by the press for their laxity in predicting the arrival of the 1651 10-Ball armada. Why hadn't the military radar installations scattered all over the world spotted the 1651 machines?

Answer: The 10-Balls, due to the peculiar gravitational-electromagnetic field enveloping them, as well as the material of the machines themselves, do not reflect radar waves. For over a month, radars had been trained on hundreds of 10-Balls, but none had ever been radar detected. The reason: The enveloping field and the machines totally absorb radar waves, hence they cannot be located by radar. Ever since World War II, the nations have striven to build bombers, planes, missiles and spacecraft that could not be spotted by radar. During the past thirty years, some progress was made in this direction by partial, but not *total* absorption of radar. Apparently the invader long ago solved the problem.

4. All over the world, it was noted, the 10-Balls periodically drop various quantities of spongy lead through their purple tubes. These faintly radioactive pellets measure from 1/2 to 1 inch. What are they?

Answer: Evidently fuel ashes. Radium, after it has given up all its energy, finally turns into lead in the final stage of its radioactive life. It is now thought that the 10-Balls use radium or atomic energy for their propulsion. There may be other forces, in addition.

It has also been observed that a 10-Ball's purple tube glows faintly green in total darkness, when hovering low. Radium and other radioactive elements, too, glow faintly green in total darkness.

5. One of the most astounding reports came from Oslo's *Norsetek University.* The invader had descended over the small house of a well-known electronics mathematician. He had been in an auto accident a month ago and had lost half of his left arm. He went through the usual forced sex ordeal, even though the stump of his arm had only partly healed. He and his wife were held for three days. They remember nothing of the two and one-half days during which they slept, or were otherwise paralyzed.

On regaining consciousness, the scientist immediately noted that his left arm had grown several inches. It has since regrown rapidly and the buds of the five future fingers already are showing. In another three weeks, the entire arm should be completely restored.

While on earth certain species such as lizards, salamanders, newts, lobsters and spiders can regrow lost tails, legs, claws—even heads may regrow in certain types—man has never been able to regenerate such organs. True, he *does* regrow teeth, skin, nails and hair (the latter if the follicle is still alive). Medicine and science so far have not succeeded in human organ regeneration, yet the invader has evidently succeeded. The Norwegian case is not an isolated one. Other reports from China, New Zealand and Peru cite similar restorations of regenerated fingers, ears, toes—an entire foot was even restored after an amputation that occurred eleven years previously.

Regeneration specialists consulted believe that the Xeno from Space has tamed cancer cells and is using them with hormone additives to regrow lost organs.

6. Observers have also noted that the purple pendant tube is a very expandable organ. Not only can it envelop a large villa, but it can also easily expand to take in a large palace of four hundred rooms, as it did in one case in England.

It is now thought that the tube is not a flexible appendage but that, when it must expand, sufficient new material descends from the top ball to meet all the necessary requirements. Such extra material probably is returned to the top later.

7. As had been observed since the very first day of the invasion, no clouds ever obscure a 10-Ball anywhere in the world. None can come closer than about half a mile distant from the 10-Ball. The energy field surrounding the machine

effectively keeps all clouds away. Even if an overcast is several miles thick, the cloud cover is completely dissipated all the way up.

Airplanes and airobiles now routinely ascend or descend through "10-Ball circular cloud holes" which give the pilots total visibility. As long as they do not come closer than half a mile to the invader's machine, there is no difficulty. If they come closer, they collide with an almost solid wall and disintegrate. The gravito-electromagnetic shield extends completely around the 10-Ball.

The invader without a doubt has solved what we would call weather control. It has been observed that their machines are not affected in the slightest degree by hurricanes, typhoons, rain, hail or snow. None of these come closer than half a mile—there is always blue sky all around. The 10-Ball does not move even a foot during the most severe atmospheric disturbance. When there is no wind on a rainy day, it is always a curious sight to see a half mile circular spot below a 10-Ball where not a drop of rain falls. Meteorologists naturally are now deep in their artificial weather control studies, since they have complete proof that weather *can* be regulated.

8. Another interesting phenomenon has been seen a number of times. It has been reported by space transports near the poles as well as by passenger *atomjets* near the equator.

The phenomenon is *full scale lightning* several miles long. It always comes from the invisible edge or the outside of the force field several hundred feet from the 10-Ball proper. The lightning bolt, it seems, can be directed anywhere, in any direction. Three weeks after the invasion, a French navy atomplane was flying in the direction of a 10-Ball. Within two miles of the force field, a lightning bolt reached out and struck the right wing of the plane, fusing about six inches of it.

Since then, all air and space flights have been ordered not to come nearer than three miles to any 10-Ball.

This seems to be only one form of armament of the invader—there are certain to be others, not discovered so far.

9. The most disturbing feature of the whole invasion, so far, and one which has caused great concern among authorities and scientists, occurred on the twenty-ninth day of the occupation.

Suddenly on that day, great masses of 10-Balls appeared over all the great inland lakes of the earth. These included five American ones: Lake Superior, Lake Michigan, Lake Huron, Lake Erie and Lake Ontario (110 machines). The Canadian Great Bear and Great Slave (40 machines). The Russian Black Sea, Caspian Sea and Lake Baikal (160 machines). The African Lake Victoria and Lake Tanganyika (50 machines). There was a total of 360 10-Ball machines.

Within a few days, the level of all of these lakes had begun to sink. It was calculated that if the same rate of depletion continued, in one year the level would be lowered five feet.

What had happened? It is plain that we have here a gigantic pumping operation, so large that it staggers the imagination. The 360 10-Balls are spaced equidistantly over all the lakes. The purple tube descends below the water level and while the machine hovers, the pumping goes on. The nine revolving balls now spin so furiously that one can hardly see them—they must lift up thousands of tons of water. Through long distance submerged audio magnifiers four miles away, one can distinctly hear the powerful sucking-pumping noises.

It is difficult for non-technicians to understand the

magnitude of this colossal operation and how much water will be lost in a year—more than flows over Niagara Falls in eight years. Havoc will be created in certain shipping areas because of the lowering of lake and river levels. Many rivers will no longer be navigable and will have to be dredged to allow ships to pass.

To get a btter idea of the vast amount of water—522-3/4 trillion gallons—that will be taken from all the lakes in a single year, let us assume that 1,000 gallons cost 30¢, which is the average cost in American homes. At that rate, *156-3/4 billions of dollars worth* of water will have been appropriated by the Xenos!

What puzzled the scientists most was the problem of where all these trillions of gallons of water went. Under close visual observation—three to four miles from a 10-Ball and with the most up-to-date *electronoptical telescopes*—nothing whatever could be discerned: no water mists, no haze, no fog even with a brilliant, blue sky overhead. But it was patent that the 10-Balls were there for only one purpose—to acquire water.

Plainly, the 10-Balls could not use it themselves. The water pumped up in less than one thousandth of a second would have swamped more than 100 Balls!

There was only one place it could go—from the earth, out into space. This was quickly confirmed by all our large radio-telescopes, which on the same day—the twenty-ninth of the invasion—detected a new exceedingly strong quasi-optical sub-micro wave formation, such as had never been observed before. Moreover, all the radio beams were directed by the pumping 10-Balls toward the magnetic North Pole, where they merged.

Thence, the radio-telescopes quickly noted, the combined beam left the earth into the region toward the North Star.

The inescapable conclusion: THE MILLIONS OF TONS OF EARTH WATER WERE TRANSMUTED DAILY INTO ELECTRO- MAGNETIC WAVES, THEN RADIATED OUT INTO SPACE TO THE HOME OF THE INVADER, THERE TO BE RECONVERTED INTO WATER.

Could the earth continue to take such vast, irretrievable loss of water? The answer would depend upon the length of time the pumping was to last.

Our scientists were interested, too, in noting that the invader did not use sea water, only salt-free, fresh lake water. The reason is obvious. It saves the invader the large amounts of extra energy needed to desalt sea water in his transmutation or converting process.

10. Contrary to all previous opinions, the invader is not solely concerned with sex research, although this seems to have been one of the first items on his agenda. The reason will be made clear in this report. Practically all scientists are now convinced that the invader is *not* a member of the mammalian family. Hence his preoccupation with human sex in all its phases. Scientists are continuously amazed how far-reaching this research is.

The Xeno from Space has gone into every facet of sex—a veritable Kinsey research! As one scientist remarked, the invader must have copies of, or has recorded, every sexological volume in every language. Thus he has lowered his 10-Balls over houses which are known to harbor male homosexuals, lesbians, masochists, transvestites and others. He has processed fully tenanted bordellos in a number of continents. He has closely studied most aborigines still peopling certain remote regions. He has visited many Eskimo homes and witnessed their ancient habit of wife loaning and wife swapping. It is doubtful if he has missed any sex deviation or aberration.

He has investigated several dozen Arabian harems in

North Africa and in the Near East. In one case, a sultan with an establishment of six wives was forced into continuous union with all his wives over a period of four hours. Ordinarily, of course, in such harems, the wives are rotated, often days or weeks apart, depending upon the virility and libido of the male and his consorts. Owners of harems are, after all, not really "sex athletes."

In the case reported, Sultan "Ibn X," a powerful man in his forties, had a heart defect. Unfortunately, at the end of his long enforced orgy, he died in his sleep, the invader's sole sex casualty to date.

In a way, this was a sort of blessing in disguise. In most other harem assaults by the invader, the end results were disastrous for some of the staff, particularly the eunuchs. Contrary to popular opinion, these emasculated wretches are not impotent by any means, although, due to the amputation of their testes, they are infertile and hence cannot reproduce. Indeed, many fully matured eunuchs can be more virile and potent than their lord and master.

When several 10-Balls descended over the harems of some elderly sultans or rulers, they could no longer satisfy all their wives in a short space of time. The eunuchs were also part of the harem and therefore they, too, came under the same devastating influence of the powerful aphrodisiac gas. Hence, there was a multiplicity of orgies that, coupled with zero gravity, turned each harem into a shambles.

In one case, after the departure of the 10-Ball, the wrath of the ruler—inflamed by his own lack of potency, plus the shameless conduct of his eunuchs and his unreasoning jealousy against his wives, who permitted themselves to be raped by the half-men—knew no bounds. He personally shot four eunuchs and three wives, entirely disregarding the fact that it was not their fault, since the influence of the invader's gas was quite irresistible.

THE

X-RACE

As a Nobel prizewinner, Duke Dubois was frequently asked to the White House to sit in on conferences to discuss ways and means of countering some of the actions of the invaders.

After the second month of the invasion, it had become crystal clear to all nations, particularly to The Big 5, that all our prime war machines and implements, from the H-bomb down, had been relegated to the status of children's toys. The world press had a holiday depicting our impotence against the Xenos, particularly in ludicrous and scathing cartoons.

A favorite one pictured an emaciated Mars, the god of war, with a huge pile of A- and H-bombs to his rear, while in the foreground there were the latest *Self-Guiding Pin-*

point Missiles--SGPM's. On Mars' lap rested a crate of apples, while in his hand was a tin cup. The public was passing by without noticing him. The caption: "An apple a day keeps the war away."

Others ran in a similar vein, all ridiculing war and armaments, and usually picturing a 10-Ball-shaped man in the background, laughing uproariously at The Big 5.

This flood of biting satire spurred the peace factions of the earth to intense activity. They made an all-out assault on The Big 5, claiming that now was the time for total disarmament. Never again would the nations be in such an advantageous position, they argued, where war could be outlawed forever.

Most of the dedicated peace advocates used this attractive theme: since the Xenos were here to stay, why not disarm completely *now* and use the tremendous armament sums for bettering the lot of the human race?

The Big 5, stung by these never-ending and derisive blasts against their defense impotence in the press, the radio and television, promised they would act soon. Indeed, there were a number of full-dress top conferences larded with important-sounding resolutions. But actually nothing came of them.

The position of The Big 5 governments was strengthened when the invader's colossal "Water Expropriation"--which the public called water robbery--showed signs of being permanent. The governments released a huge propaganda barrage against the peace advocates, painting a dire picture of the future and predicting how, in the end, humanity would die of thirst. Actually, "in the end" might be many years away--if at all--but that fact was not publicized.

The majority of the public was lulled by the fact that The Big 5 now had mutually binding treaties pledging that for the duration of the invasion there would never be a man-made war, and by the feeling that "things would in the end work themselves out automatically," particularly since all armament was now outdated and completely outclassed.

This more or less logical reasoning took much of the starch out of the arguments of the advocates of disarmament. They were left without a convincing counterbarrage, the more so because people realized that, with a continuous depletion of our fresh water supply, a new and dangerous world emergency had arisen which somehow must be met soon.

The Big 5 were in no mood to disarm. In view of the constantly listening-in Xenos, this could not very well be publicized. But in the government secret underground rooms, there were constant conferences of the foremost military technicians of the world. And invariably the chief topic was: *How to beat the invader.* Whether the conferences were on a national or international level, the subject rarely changed. "We must best the Xenos!"

It was, unfortunately, also true that during such international conferences of top scientists and technicians, the only information that was ever exchanged was always "old hat." The ways of the humans had not changed much even with the invasion. The old rivalries and jealousies remained. If any advances and breakthroughs occurred in one camp, they were kept secret until the other caught up with them, as they invariably did.

Scientific and technological progress evolves in an organized growth, nearly always moving ahead in an orderly fashion—it never advances in leaps. When one scientist is working on a problem, usually—unknown to him—someone else is working on the same problem in another part of the world. Often they solve it simultaneously.

When Alexander Graham Bell invented the telephone, his patent attorney presented his patent application on February 14, 1876, to the U.S. Patent Office. On the very same day, two hours later, Elisha Gray presented *his* patent application for a telephone to the U.S. Patent Office, too. Both telephones were almost identical, yet both inventors had never seen each other, had never even known of the other's existence.

So, too, with war inventions—they seldom occur in isolation. Usually what one nation has, the others will soon have, too. It is true, however, that the same ideas may not be *perfected* simultaneously, because one nation may not think favorably of a given invention, while another does.

This was the case in World War II. Although the Germans came out first with their famous V1 and V2 rocket bombs, there was nothing new about them. Their rocket expert, the great Professor Hermann Oberth, had written a most comprehensive book on retroaction and rocketry in 1923. (He became one of the chief German V1 and V2 technicians at Pennemunde during World War II.) The other nations all had the book, but didn't think much of rockets at the time. Even long after that, the Americans did not see the rocket handwriting in the sky until they woke up on October 4, 1957, to find that the Russians had placed the first man-made satellite in orbit.

As the world became more and more alarmed by the Xeno invasion, particularly by the invader's depletion of the earth's irreplaceable fresh water in the great lakes of the earth, Dubois was called again to the White House by Hector Farragut.

In the elaborate presidential secret underground room, Farragut had assembled twenty-odd leading U.S. scientists and military men to weigh anew the problem of how to cope with the invader.

The military, since the first day of the invasion, had been obsessed with the urge to "bring down a 10-Ball" in order to explore its secrets. Yet they had no concrete strategy to present.

In former sessions, there had been plans presented of super ultrasound bombs, cosmic A and Z bombs—the latter "secret" with the U. S. forces.

One was a plan to equip certain cities with huge tanks of chloroform (or similar narcotic gases). Then, when a 10-Ball descended over a house in that city, the special gas was to be diverted into the city's regular gas mains. Citizens about to be kidnaped would quickly open their gas burners, freeing the narcotic gases. These gases would then go up through the purple tube and render the Xenos unconscious.

Actually, this plan was never seriously considered, but it was thought that a similar, better plan might work. The idea was to drop upon the 10-Balls quantities of transparent balls containing concentrated narcotics from a great height by means of some of our huge atom-hovering transports. The transparent plastic balls would burst when they struck the surrounding force field, thus liberating the gas which would envelop the 10-ball. It was thought that the gas would then reach the inside of the 10-Ball, rendering the Xenos unconscious. This idea was abandoned when it was discovered that the invaders wore helmets and that they did not breathe the earth's atmosphere for fear of germs and viruses. It was certain that they manufactured their own "air," because in outer space, through which they came, there is only a vast and total vacuum. It was known, too, by actual telescopic observation that none of the 10-Balls making up a machine had any windows or other openings. Hence no gas from outside could ever get inside the balls. Even if it entered the purple tube, the Xenos' air locks would keep it from the interior of the top ball.

During the presidential conference, a number of other plans were presented by the military, but all were declared unworkable by the scientists. At this point, President Farragut called on Dubois, who had been uncommunicative so far, to present his ideas on the subject.

"Mr. President," Dubois began, "may I say that in this instance there does not seem to be any feasible plan that we can evolve. Indeed, it would seem to me that even were such a plan possible, which I personally doubt, it would go for naught.

"Let us suppose for a moment that, by some lucky accident, a 10-Ball were to become disabled and come down, reasonably intact. The Xenos, let us also suppose, have been killed. Now we have the 10-Ball and can get at its secrets.

"Mr. President, it is my considered opinion, and that of many of my associates, that we would learn very little from our lucky acquisition and that at best it would take many years before we could make much headway.

"Let me put it this way: Imagine that we could hand the illustrious Archimedes, the greatest scientist of his age, 2,250 years ago, a modern *TV-wristime*,* or a pocket *transistoradio-lighter*. What could he learn from them, even if he had the necessary tools to take them apart? Mighty little. He would have no idea whatsoever of radio and television. The miniscule parts would no doubt astonish and intrigue him, but he could not form an opinion of the mechanism and its possible uses. *Over 2,000 years of experience and technical progress separate us from him.*

"As the passage of time goes, that is a very short period. Now we are confronted with the 10-Balls, built by a civilization that may separate us from them by a minimum

*A TV-wristime catches signals from a special TV-timestation. It is not a watch, but gives time on its dial via television.

of 500,000 to 1 million years, according to the estimates of our foremost thinkers. So what is to be gained by taking one of their machines apart? Nothing, absolutely nothing for perhaps centuries. You might as well put a chimpanzee in charge—even the most intelligent—of the latest H-atomelectronic generating plant and expect him to operate it!

"If we persist in our hopeless and totally inadequate schemes to annoy or molest a highly civilized—and evidently peaceful—race, we are certain to reap a whirlwind of disasters.

"It is as if a large anthill were to attack humanity today. The result would be ludicrously one-sided for the unhappy ants.

"Mr. President, I would counsel that we desist from all thought of attacking the X-Race. No good can come of it. We must bear with the invader in good grace, as we must bear with a hard winter. Right now there is absolutely nothing that we can do about either."

There was a long and painful pause. Then the President slowly rose and declared the meeting adjourned. In deep thought, the men filed out in silence.

* * *

At the end of the second month of the invasion, Dubois was giving his now historic lecture on the invader in the mammoth 75,000-seat *amphiarena* in Chicago. Recently completed, this superb public palace was immense in every sense. It was at once a theater, an opera house, a sports stadium, an exhibition hall, a hippodrome, an *aquatorium*, a political convention forum, a skating arena, a supercenter for every imaginable function. The structure was so designed that the space under the seats on one side became the stage of a huge motion picture theater. Thus several separate performances could be given at the same time in the amphiarena without one interfering with the other.

The amphiarena could revolve on its axis on giant *tungmolyb* bearings, many of which were motorized. Thus the whole Brobdingnagian building could follow the sun, a most important feature during sports events. If rain or snow threatened, three sides of the arena, normally open, could be closed in minutes by means of iris-type closures.

There was a huge superstructure on top of the amphiarena. This was the Chicago Heliport, where all helicopters landed and took off. Below the basement, under the steel beams supporting the whole structure, there was a mammoth garage for many thousand cars.

For the occasion of Dubois' talk, one of the huge stages had the latest model *linguaverters,* an electronic brain which converts ten languages *simultaneously.* As Dubois talked in English, the world's ten principal languages were broadcast simultaneously from *Denver's International World Station,* which supplied American news all over the world, and even to the moon. The ten languages were: English, French, Spanish, German, Russian, Italian, Chinese (Mandarin), Hindi (India Moslem), Arabic and Portuguese.

The entire amphiarena was *auto-aircontrolled* on this hot August night—even the part that was open. This was achieved by powerful jets of refrigerated air, forced out at high speed from nozzles. These air-curtains shut off the outside air effectively from the inside, and they were so powerful that even a wind of thirty miles could not blow the refrigerated air currents aside. Hence, the inside of the entire arena was kept cool. Near the ceiling were other horizontal refrigerated *air-curtains,* some with "air-openings" to allow the rising hot air from the arena to drift upward into the outer air.

There had been an immense interest in the Xenos—or the X-Race, as they were called—and Dubois had been importuned by the entire world press to inform the people of the latest pronouncements of science, the origin of the race, its habitat and any other intelligence that could be disclosed at this time.

The following is a condensed version of Professor Duke Dubois' talk:

My Friends of the World:

You have asked me a multitude of interesting questions about our friends, the X-Race.

One question has come from several hundred people, and I can answer it in the affirmative. The question: "Are the Xenos *X-Heads*?" The answer to this bad pun is, "Yes!" (Laughter).

Most other serious questions we cannot as yet answer, because, unfortunately, so far we have no means of communicating with the invader, but we hope some day we will.

One of the reasons, we surmise, is that the Xenos think so lightningly fast that we could never follow them. It is quite possible that during their long evolution—500,000 to 1 million years ahead of ours—their thinking processes have speeded up at such a rate that they can read 100,000 words in seconds. This need not astonish you—take our modern electronic computers. They can do 660,000 operations, that is calculations, per second.*

More likely there is another reason—why should they talk to *us*? Do we talk to bugs or worms or termites? The X-Race are so far above us in evolution that it would be idiotic for them to lower themselves to communicating with us. Besides, it would be a total loss of time—what could they learn by talking to us? We really should know our place and act accordingly.

Do we talk to grasshoppers or ants when we study them? All we wish to know is what makes them tick, how they live,

*The IBM-7090 (fully transistorized data processing system) performs 210,000 additions or subtractions in *one* second. (1959 information courtesy International Business Machines, New York.)

how they propagate.

Why don't the Xenos descend from their 10-Balls and walk among us?

The answer is simple. The X-Race are not of terrestrial origin. Of this all scientists are convinced today. We know from direct evidence that they cannot live in our atmosphere. The air pressure is probably far too high for them here. Hence, they must wear special pressurized suits when they investigate and examine us. They may live in a world where radiation is high. Here on earth, with little radiation, they probably could not survive. Moreover, our microbes and viruses would surely kill them in short order. *Even sunlight may be fatal to them.* Eyewitnesses who glimpsed them in their top ball noted that they worked almost in darkness—in a faint green phosphorescence.

Walk around on earth? We are convinced they can't. They are probably very frail, used to a greatly reduced gravity, such as exists on a very small planet, where you or I would not weigh more than three pounds each. Hence, while "walking" on earth, they would collapse in a heap, never to get up again. We know this reasoning to be correct because the only two earth people—who were not paralyzed in the top ball—noted that the Xenos were working in zero gravity. And that is why they will never walk among us.

What incredible energy or forces do they use? This is a question that is asked quite frequently. Let us remember that humanity has known real energy only for a few hundred short years, in a history going back almost a million years. The first practical steam engine has been known only about 300 years, the first practical electric motor only a short 120 years. The first atomic reactor has only been known since 1945, a paltry 51 years—and even today our atomic energy plants are so crude that despite the atom's inherent colossal energy, we can only extract a small percentage of it, the rest being waste.

But there are far more powerful sources of energy that we have hardly even tapped. Cosmic energy is one, anti-matter energy another. Many scientists are now convinced that the Xenos' nine revolving balls are anti-matter propelled— physicists call it a mass-energy. How they do it is, of course, totally unknown.

What can we tell you of the very extensive sex research of the X-Race? As we have publicized repeatedly, the Xenos probably are not of the mammalian race. They know that we evolved to be the ruling species of all living creatures in our world and are dominant because we can think and reason. Hence, the X-Race center their research on us, rather than, say, the whale, the largest of all earth creatures.

The Xenos, too, are probably the ruling creatures of their world. They, too, think and reason as we know only too well. Hence, they wish to ascertain exactly *what* it is that made *us* rise to the top. What makes a thinking, reasoning creature? Curiously enough, we ourselves do not know.

Why didn't the dinosaurs, who also walked on two feet, become the dominant race? Why not the whale? We don't know the reason.

What has sex to do with all this? In sex research you must go back to the beginning of a race or species. Even before the spermatozoon or the ovum is created, there are forces at work of which we humans know little so far. Under the most powerful microscope the human sperm and the pig's sperm look exactly alike, yet they grow up into vastly different species. Why? We glibly say heredity, but that, again, begs the question. Frankly, we don't know the whole answer. If anyone does today, it is probably the Xenos. Some scientists believe that by slightly altering a sperm, be it human or that of some other mammal, either by chemicals or radiation or some other still unknown means, an entirely different species can be created—and probably will in the future. It is even possible in this manner to create a superhuman race. Time will tell.

In the meanwhile, the X-Race in their sex research are learning a thousand facets of the human race, which are most probably new and strange to them and which they wish to record scientifically.

Human scientists work in a similar vein. They have observed the ants for thousands of years, although there is not yet in existence an *accurate* step-by-step record of the nuptial flight of a queen ant and her chosen male drone. Few entomologists have ever been close enough to witness the entire action.

Where does the X-Race come from? We do not know whether they originate in the solar system or in some other part of the universe. Because the converted water beam which they transmit in the direction of the North Star seems to fall beyond the solar system, scientists presume that their habitat must belong to a not-too-distant star that has a similar planetary system to our own. But this is pure conjecture.

Our universe abounds with so many surprises that literally anything is possible. Our nearest star, *Alpha Centauri,* is four light years away. Yet it is possible that there is a closer *extinct* star nearer to us. We can't see it or detect it because it may be a dead, extinguished sun. *But that is no reason why it could not have its own planetary system.* In that system there could be a minor planet, the home of the Xenos. The outside of such a planet, not heated by a dark, lifeless sun, would be as cold as interstellar space. Yet if it contained a sufficient amount of uranium or other radioactive element, the inside could be quite warm and livable. The interior of the earth, too, as we know now, is heated to a degree by uranium. Hence, if the Xenos' planet were partly hollow, there is no reason why they could not thrive in the interior of their little world. We know already that they do not require light, hence their abode most likely is a dark one.

But *what* are the Xenos, if they are non-mammals?

Again, our assertion that the X-Race is not mammalian is purely conjecture.

We originally concluded, because of their extensive sex research, that the Xenos could *not* be constituted like us. If, we reasoned, they were mammalian, they could not possibly be so interested in us and extend their sex research into so many avenues.

On the other hand, what is a mammal? One that is a vertebrate, the female of which has milk-secreting glands for feeding offspring. Yet the platypus, also a mammal, lays eggs and has no milk-secreting glands. It does not suckle its young, as does a true mammal. So you see, there are mammals *and* mammals.

This brings us to the X-Race. Most scientists, including

myself, strongly feel that the Xenos are akin to the insect species, although, not originating on our earth, they probably are not true insects, any more than a platypus is a true mammal.

When we try to classify an extraterrestrial species, our thinking is often circumscribed by our knowledge of comparative earth creatures. This makes no sense or logic, because evolution on another world may take totally unknown and unforeseen directions.

We are further handicapped by the fact that we have never seen a Xeno in full light. All the facts we have—if facts they be—are that a Xeno seems to have two enormous eyes (or eyelike organs) and four armlike appendages. Since all these organs were totally enclosed, we are by no means certain that they did not belong to robots.

But let us suppose that what was glimpsed in the vague green effluvium actually was a live Xeno. What does this prove? The four arms—no legs were seen—would appear insect-like, but that is all the "proof" we have. A very slim clue. We are in total darkness about the head, which, judging by the helmet enclosure, must be large. From here on, everything is speculative.

Nature, in its multitudinous ways, is so prolific that literally anything is possible in her creations. It is probable that creatures with both mammal and insect characteristics exist. On the basis of our scant, vaporous evidence, the Xeno could be one of a thousand different types of fantastic beings. Every one of them *could* exist somewhere on one of the billions of worlds in our incomprehensible, huge universe. There is no limit to complex creatures, even on our own earth. Multiply this by billions of other worlds, where physical conditions vary enormously, and we must come to the conclusion that literally the most phantasmagorical animates must exist on some far distant planet.

We thus must come to the inescapable conclusion that no matter how alien we feel the Xenos could be, when we finally do come face to face with one of them, we will find that the X-Race will likely be even more grotesque than we had calculated.

Finally, how do the Xenos communicate with each other? Obviously, the 1,600-odd 10-Ball craft hovering and traveling over the earth must be in constant communication with each other. That seems elementary.

Moreover, they must also have some means of exchanging intelligence with their distant home base, or at least with relays along the route which they have come.

Yet, so far, despite all of our most energetic efforts to intercept their messages, we have drawn a complete blank. Why?

We are much too backward to cope with the highly sophisticated means of communication which, no doubt, the Xenos have evolved. Let us remember that it was only ninety-five years ago—in 1901—that Marconi sent his famous letter "S" signal across the Atlantic via wireless to inaugurate the era of long distance radio communication.

It was only yesterday, fifty years ago, in 1946, that the U.S. Signal Corps sent the first radio signal to the moon, 238,000 miles away, and received it back 2.4 seconds later.*

Thus, we can see that we are mere tyros at the complex art of communication.

Is it possible that the Xenos communicate by means of telepathy or similar means? We do not know. If they do, we certainly have no instruments to intercept telepathic waves—if waves they are. So far we have evolved no *telepathic detector,* and that is precisely why so many scientists are still skeptical about telepathy.

Yet we know that even on our own earth many creatures communicate with each other by some means. Ants, moths and other species seem to be able to exchange information with each other at a distance. As to how they do it, we have only guesses, no actual scientific facts.

The future, we are convinced, will unlock this vast and fascinating domain. Until that time arrives, we must continue to grope in the realm of all-enveloping darkness on the subject of *Total Communication.*

*The author of this volume had predicted the exact event 19 years before the actual event in his article "Can We Radio the Planets?" in the February, 1927, issue of *Radio News.* He forecast the time at 2-1/2 seconds—an error of 1/10 of a second.

7

LUNAR

ELDORADO

Near the fifth month of the Xeno earth invasion the world's paplast press reported increasing restlessness among the population everywhere.

No one could assign the exact reason for this feeling, as the occupation was certainly peaceful enough. Outside of the sexual research projects of the Xenos—which, incidentally, by this time was just as much championed by half of the earth's population as it was fiercely resented by the other half—the masses instinctively were never entirely at ease.

There was always in their consciousness the terrorizing threat that the invader was ever poised to vaporize humanity.

This universal feeling was most accurately expressed in

the single question now being voiced by all and splashed over the daily papers: "What are the Xenos *really* up to?" The masses did not feel for a second that the invaders had descended on the world for the single purpose of sex research on humans. They instinctively felt that a great invasion fleet of over 1,600 huge machines doesn't travel billions of miles, or displace itself in space and time, just to study a few thousand—to them—barbaric and backward humans! There was also the gigantic "water steal" of the earth's great inland lakes that certainly did not augur well for the future. Hence, the more and more impatient question, "What next?"

At this precise time the Xenos abruptly stopped their sex research on married (or unmarried) couples and concentrated on homosexuality. It is impossible to ascertain exactly how the invaders knew where to find homosexuals—of both sexes—but with their uncanny, all-knowing means of scientific detection, they seemed to have little difficulty in locating their quarry. The popular feeling was that the Xenos did all their "sleuthing" and spying via telepathy, but scientists were not certain that this was the sole explanation.

The methods of investigating homosexuals closely paralleled the pattern of studying heterosexual couples, except that the detention period rarely exceeded twenty-four hours. The Xenos used the same aphrodisiac gas treatment and did the same sex punctures. On these particular males and females, however, there were no punctures inside the arm crux.

However, there was one interesting change. In addition to the usual sex punctures over the abdomen of the females and the epididymis of the males, both sexes were given one additional puncture in back of the hairline above the forehead.

Scientists guessed that, inasmuch as homosexuality may be a purely mental state, the Xenos made certain cerebral investigations in order to satisfy themselves as to what actually causes homosexuality. It was also quickly ascertained that the head puncture went right through the osseous part of the cranium, but did no damage of any kind.

* * *

One evening after dinner, a short time after these events, during the fifth month of the invasion, Duke Dubois and Donny were talking "invasion-shop." This did not happen frequently, as Dubois now was constantly harassed by meetings with his scientist-confrères, endless lectures, government conferences and dozens of other time-consuming duties, so that there remained little home life for the couple during those arduous times.

But this was their wedding anniversary and they had chosen to spend the evening together and strictly alone.

"I am giving an after-luncheon talk next week to the 8,400 members of the American Ladies Space Club,* via *'locked' TV-phantomcast,"*** began Donny, "and I want you to brief me on a few points and bring me up to date on several others."

*To become a member, a woman must have traveled as a pilot or technician in space above the terrestrial atmosphere, or have made an actual worthwhile contribution to space flight.

**"Locked" TV, a 1970 television improvement, is in principle similar to the old "closed-circuit" TV. In other words, it is "private," although broadcast all over the world via four space satellites, which gravitate above the earth. Your TV set must have a special "key," otherwise the picture on your set is "scrambled." You obtain the "key"—a special punched card—from your government, upon proper identification. Certain "locked broadcasts" are only for certain countries. A *phantomcast* projects *live* phantom-images so that the picture appears about six feet from your TV set. In this manner, a speaker can be projected into the center of your living room. While only an illusion, it is a very effective one.

For technical details, see the February, 1958, issue of *Radio-Electronics*, page 31.

"Fine," said Duke, "ask away."

"How long do you and your associates think this invasion is likely to last?"

"That is quite impossible to foretell; no one actually has a basis for such a prediction."

"Well, then, where does their food come from? As far as we know, they don't even take on water—except for the few hundred 10-Balls hovering over the lakes—and they don't ever eject any waste, either, except a few lead pellets. So they can't stay here forever!"

"Well, well," Duke laughed. "As a Space Club member, you should be able to answer that one yourself. How will our Jupiter expedition, which started out nearly a year ago, survive? Since, as you know, humans can't possibly land on Jupiter, they must return after circumnavigating the gaseous planet, an overall trip of two years. They could, of course, land on one of the 12 Jupiter moons in an emergency, but the plans of the expedition do not call for this.

"As you ought to know," Duke continued, "when traveling in space, we must reuse *everything* we require biologically—the air we breathe, even our own wastes. In space you can't throw anything out—it would only gravitate around the spaceship and mire up the thick glass observation panes. Food, as you also know, is chiefly grown on board from chlorella and other algae. There is also a good store of hydraulically compressed foods necessary for variety's sake and 'Sunday' dinner. But that doesn't last forever, chiefly because of lack of room. Since there is no hydraulic press in spaceships, as a rule, the reprocessed and recovered food takes more space than the original food, hence only a certain amount can be carried, if it is not to take up all available space in the ship."

"I see what you mean. So the invasion expedition of the

Xenos could last quite a few years."

"Exactly. Incidentally, a race so far advanced over ours will have its own highly sophisticated means of subsistence and survival in space that may last, if necessary, hundreds of years. On such extended voyages, travelers will live and die and new ones will be born to replace them in a continuous cycle."

"Why," asked Donny, "did the Xenos have to visit earth? Why not some other planet?"

"Who says they didn't? They may have visited Mars, for instance, before we did several years ago. For all we know, they may have visited all the other solar planets, with Mercury perhaps excepted on account of its excessive heat, caused by the proximity to the sun. All this is purely speculative, but quite possible."

"How many Xenos," Donny then asked, "do you estimate there are in the invasion fleet?"

"We have too few facts to give an exact answer to that. All we know for certain is that the top globe measures about seventy-five feet in diameter. This, presumably, is the 'bridge' of their spaceship, while the other nine revolving spheres are the propelling machinery. There must be a good deal of other apparatus—instrumentation, steering and guiding machines—in the top globe. In addition, there must be food stores, food-growing installations, food and liquids recovery means, communication mechanisms, and thousands of others, whose nature we cannot even guess. Just think of two: one, the huge pumping machinery and electronic converting gear needed to break down and transmit the water by radio to their faraway home.

"The other, the powerful invisible electromagnetic shield or whatever it is, that can even deflect an H-bomb—that machinery alone must be quite bulky. All in all, in the opinion of most scientists-engineers, more than 80 percent of the available room in the top sphere must of necessity be taken up by such equipment. That doesn't leave too much room for Xenos, granted that they are as bulky as humans. They need a certain amount of room to move around, living quarters, sleeping space and so forth. Consequently, we doubt if there are more than ten or twenty Xenos per ship—always granted that they are *live* Xenos! As I have often mentioned before, they may be robots. In that case, there may be many more, because robots don't eat, don't sleep, hence they need much less room. If we have to do with live Xenos, there may be between 15,000 and 30,000 invaders, or maybe more."

Just as Duke finished, the private *visiphone* went on. This was his direct line to the university Science Council room. Simultaneously, a red signal kept flashing. This meant: *Urgent*. Duke's assistant, Floyd Manternach, was on the screen. The *loudphone* sounded:

"Dr. Dubois, an urgent report. Two days ago the Xenos stopped their processing of the homosexuals. Today, all over the globe, they descended en masse on the primary schools, taking out as many as one hundred young children at a time. Japan and Australia, because of the time difference, sent in the first reports. The invaders keep each batch of children about six hours. Each child has two punctures beneath the hairline above the forehead. So far no one knows the significance of this."

From his chair, ten feet away from the visiphone, Dubois replied:

"O.K., Floyd, give me a bulletin every two hours during the night. I will put the visiphone on recorder while I sleep and get a better picture of new developments by 7:00 A.M. Goodnight."

For some minutes Dubois was lost in thought. Then he did some figuring on his pad.

"That's about 600 children per day, per machine. Or 720,000 children a day if only 1,200 machines are all processing together. In 30 days, if they keep that up, they will have treated over 21-1/2 million children! This far exceeds anything they have done to humans up to now. I wonder—"

"What can they be up to now?" Donny broke in. "It certainly can't be sex this time."

"No, this is something altogether different, and I doubt if it is research either. They did all the human research they needed on adults; therefore this looks like a completely new undertaking."

"But," persisted Donny, "what could it possibly be?"

"My dear," Duke observed, "let me be quite frank. Scientists are not gods and not omniscient; they are quite human. For the past few months the Xenos have shown us up in our true light—they have brought home to us what we knew all the time, namely our profound lack of knowledge. The other night at a lecture before six hundred scientists, I coined a quotation that curiously enough was roundly applauded: *Scientists know too many things that aren't so!*

"As we look back twenty-five years we laugh at what our silly beliefs were then—twenty-five years from now we shall laugh at what our beliefs and convictions were today. You see, we know so little—ask any scientist what an atom or an electron is, or magnetism, or light, or electricity. We just make learned guesses and that is about all.

"So if you ask what the Xenos are now doing to our children, I must confess I do not know. I have several ideas, but I'd rather wait until I have more information. But of one thing I *am* certain: this latest exploit of the Xenos is going to cause an unprecedented uproar in the population all over the world. Yet I have a hunch—there is little science in hunches—that the children will not be harmed, and they may even be benefited. I say this only in the light of the fact that so far the Xenos have appeared to be *very* civilized."

* * *

In the weeks that followed, extreme rioting broke out all over the world in protest over the "children's abductions," as they became known. Public schools closed down everywhere, in every country of the world.

The governments had a difficult time in quieting the rioting, yet became organized quickly after a world conference of eminent scientists, educators, physicians and other authorities had pointed out that no harm of any kind had come to the children.

Indeed, curiously enough, those children who had been "abducted" at an age of six to eight years, were the most vociferous in wanting the schools reopened. Privately, every authority who talked to these children was immediately struck with the fact that a profound change had come over these youngsters. It was difficult to pinpoint it, but they certainly appeared more intelligent than they were before.

At any rate, the public storm died down suddenly and the schools reopened again. The Xenos, who had in the meanwhile concentrated on private schools, which did stay open, resumed their "processing" of children in all public schools.

Naturally, the scientists and other specialists in the field concentrated on the children who had been "treated" by the Xenos, to ascertain just what the head punctures meant. An answer was not easy.

The children were not much help, as they universally had been placed under deep hypnosis the second the purple tube of the 10-Ball had descended over the school. Everyone instantly went to sleep and stayed rigid for six hours. This included all the teachers of both sexes, principals and all others present. The adults, however, were not processed—they stayed where they had been. The children felt nothing before or after, and by the time the purple tube had lifted, the punctures had healed completely, though less than a few hours old.

As with the homosexuals, the punctures were clean holes trephined through the skull. But unlike human trephining, the holes were less than 1/8″ in diameter. None of the children developed an infection on or near the holes.

When the schools opened once more, television sets and automatic cameras were placed in a number of schools so that authorities could "watch how the Xenos operated."

Duke Dubois laughed when this plan was first suggested, but merely said: "Watch and see."

As he had thought, exactly nothing was learned. Having been inside a purple tube once himself, he knew that the powerful electromagnetic waves of the 10-Balls at close range would put every television set out of commission, and as for photographic cameras, every foot of film was blackened.

Built-in-the-wall electronic periscopes had a similar fate. The distortion of the light rays was so severe that no picture could be obtained. Even an underground periscope going down fifty feet under a school got similar negative results.

It was not until the seventh month of the invasion that a partial answer to the Xenos' head punctures of the world's children became apparent. And the answer was only a preliminary one.

Duke Dubois, in a worldwide broadcast lecture, said:

We recently made an extensive research on several children who had had their craniums punctured by the

Xenos. These particular children, who had died from accidents, were carefully investigated and the following facts were learned.

It seems now established that the Xenos injected certain live cells into the front part of the brain in the region known as the frontal lobe. These cells have taken root in all children treated by the Xenos, and it appears that two tiny new organs about the size of a large pea will grow permanently in all treated children.

What the Xenos did is simply what horticulturists do routinely when they graft a shoot or bud of one plant—usually a superior one—into the stem of another.

It has been noted, too, that no children over the age of eight have been processed by the invaders. Evidently the graft of the new organs must take place at a certain age if it is to be successful, hence older children were not treated.

Where do these organs come from? We can only guess that they must be laboratory-grown by the Xenos from original parent cells which they cultivate as we do, let us say, yeast cells.

The burning question now before humanity: Just what are these new organs? A preliminary, yet only a partial answer is, the organs are partly super-intellect, partly telepathic.

We make this assertion after having studied intensely several thousand children processed by the Xen)s. It appears in practically all cases that these children are far more intelligent than other non-processed ones. Their I.Q. averages close to 200—what it will be in one or two years is anyone's guess. It should be borne in mind that the organs are still growing and have not reached maturity.

The telepathic ability of these children in thousands of tests is very evident, even to non-scientists. Tests will be going on for years to ascertain how much the telepathic organ can expand in efficiency and how humanity can be benefited by its use of telepathy on a grand scale. Incidentally, it has already been demonstrated that a telepathic individual can "shut off" telepathy just as you can shut your eyes if you do not wish to see.

Finally, geneticists are certain that succeeding generations will grow the new organs in time. Not every child will inherit them, but it is felt that succeeding generations may do so. Perhaps in several hundred years, most humans will have them. As yet we have not assigned a name to the new organ.

It is felt by us, the scientists of the world, that humanity should be grateful to the Xenos for having attempted to make our world a better place to live in, and we certainly should place no obstacles in the path of their improving our children, as long as they visit our earth.

Subsequently, most of the world's population seemed to share the scientists' view of the new generation's improvement of the race, but as in all things, there was a minority of dissenters.

They called it a dark plot of the invaders to shape humanity for their own purposes and designs. Why, they asked, should the Xenos be so good to us? That ran completely "against Nature," some said, while others warned, "You can't get something for nothing. There is a dark and sinister motive behind all this." What all this was, however, they did not venture to guess.

Duke Dubois had an answer to much of this negative thinking. In his opinion, the Xenos, as super-civilized beings, obtained a certain amount of satisfaction from accomplishment, just as the renowned botanist genius, Luther Burbank, did from breeding a long series of "new creations" in vegetables—the famed Burbank potato, and fruits, flowers, grains and grasses such as the world had never seen before. Said Burbank, "I shall be content if because of me, there shall be better fruits and fairer flowers."

* * *

It was in the seventh month of the Xenos' invasion that sudden word was flashed from the moon that it had been invaded by forty machines much like the 10-Balls but larger. Instead of ten balls, there were ten half-balls, and half-cones; that is, the shape was ball-like at the bottom, with a sharp cone on top.

The forty *10-Ball-Cone Machines*, as they soon were dubbed, settled over the moon in formation in a small crater and started operations near the north pole.

This particular crater, nearly sixty miles in diameter, was bisected by the American and Russian sectors.

When, in 1975, The Big-5 nations had landed on the moon, they had laid out a plan of division that looked roughly like a peeled orange. Running from pole to pole there were eight orange-like "slices." These were the American, Russian, English, French and Japanese sectors, and three unassigned ones. The latter three were to be assigned to other nations as they arrived in space machines of their own manufacture.

The eight sectors covered the whole of the surface of the moon visible from earth. Exactly the same division was made of the opposite side of the moon, which is never seen from earth. There were, therefore, altogether sixteen sectors dividing up the entire moon. Property rights of the various nations extended down, "orange-wedge-shaped-like," toward the axis of the moon.

This was important because our satellite is a world strewn with practically extinct volcanos. Most of these have large, tortuous flues or chimneys extending for miles down into the moon's interior. Many of them branch out into huge caverns. This is not only a spelunker's paradise, but a treasure world unparalleled anywhere on earth.

Every mineral you can think of is found here—gold, silver, platinum, nickel, copper and the rest; in addition, radioactive ore and rare earths* of every imaginable

*The term "rare earths," a misnomer on the moon, has recently been changed to "rare selenites" (*selene*, the moon).

variety, such as uranium, thorium and many others abound, as well as diamonds and other gems.

No wonder, then, that the world's nations were falling all over each other in their attempt to exploit the moon. During the past few years, huge mining complexes had appeared all over the surface of our satellite. Airtight buildings had been erected everywhere, fully air-conditioned as well as heated. As the moon has no atmosphere, it is really immersed in a vacuum in which no man can exist unless he wears a space suit.

Man still must wear one when he works in the moon's interior, because in the caves or mines there is no air, either.

Although a 150-pound man weighs only 24-3/4 pounds here, life on the moon, nevertheless, is not a picnic. During the long lunar day, the fierce solar heat near the equator may reach 300° F. During the long night, it drops to -250° F.

Power supply on the moon is no problem. Huge banks of recently perfected *solaradioactive* cells convert over 75 percent of the sun's energy into electricity. At night *cosmigenerators* take over for light and heat, as the mines are not worked continuously. (The moon day lasts fourteen earth days, as does the lunar night.)

In order to get free sun-electricity at all times, the nations are now installing electric power lines that run from one side of the moon to the other. As each side of the moon is in full sunlight fourteen earth days, and as both sides will have a full installation of solaradioactive cells, there will be a continuous power supply for all plants. Such power is literally free, except for maintenance charges. This makes for an ideal economic setup.

All mineral ores are processed into metals on the moon directly at the mines. It would not pay to move the heavy ores to the earth—the transportation cost via space machines would be prohibitive; in addition, smelting on the moon is far less costly than on earth.

*   *   *

It took several weeks before the humans on the moon grasped what was going on after the Xenos had invaded the Russian and American sectors so unceremoniously. Not that the two nations could have done anything about it anyway.

They were happy that the Xenos' mining operations were inside a small crater that neither nation was exploiting at the time; in this manner the three interests did not interfere with each other.

But what were the Xenos mining? Why couldn't they do it on earth? And why the ball-cone machines that were 25 percent larger than those used on earth?

The answers did not come at once. Indeed, it was not known for some time *what* they were mining. Only later was it discovered that they were mining a rare ore six miles down which had never been found on earth—as far as is known, it doesn't exist on earth at all. It is now known as element 116, *Lunium*—named for our satellite—a rather unstable radioactive metalloid.

How did the Xenos know it was there? As it is very radioactive, it would appear that they had detected it long ago during an exploration trip with their hypersensitive instruments and then returned to mine it. It seems to be very rare, but for some reason essential to the Xenos.

It was a team of Americans that found out quite by accident what they *did* with it. One day, shortly after the Xenos invaded the moon, the Americans were flying a few miles from the lunar north pole in their small space-mapping ship.

Suddenly, all metallic objects started to glow with a green phosphorescence. Simultaneously, everything—even their whole craft—became radioactive. Veering hastily away from the pole, they returned to their base to be decontaminated.

Luckily, they had not absorbed a fatal dose of radiation. Now they began to understand why the Xenos had cones on their "mining" units. These cones glowed fiercely green in the long lunar night, and all of them pointed to Polaris, the pole star in the north.

A team of physicists and electronic engineers hastily summoned from the earth pieced the puzzle together as follows:

The Xenos, through their purple tubes, probably sent robots down into the lunar crater to mine the radioactive ore. This was processed on the spot, then electronically transmuted into electromagnetic waves. Thence it was radiated into space in a manner similar to the way they converted water into radio waves. The cones were actually directional aerials.

There was, however, a big difference from their water transmission. The radio waves were radioactive, too, a new principle in physics never before known to science.

After the three Americans in their spaceship blundered upon the edge of the Xenos' deadly radioactive radio beam, all space patrols were warned to give the beam a wide berth.

The nature of the Xenos' mining operations had been discovered, but the big question remained: What did they do with this radioactive element when they recombined it at their own abode?

ELECTRONIC

SOIRÉE

An extraordinary cosmic event took place during the seventh month of the Xenos' invasion, which shook the world almost as much as their earth occupation itself.

Humanity, used to space travel, space invasion by an alien race and dozens of new man-made wonders, by the first month of 1997, had become so blasé that only the most spectacular event could excite it.

But on January 10, 1997, a wondrous new celestial object appeared in the sky, not an artificial man-made satellite that you could glimpse only by means of opera glasses or telescope, but a moon, apparently as large as our old standby Luna.

It wasn't round, but oblong and—most unusual of all—it traveled in a retrograde motion. That is, it rose in the west and set in the east. It really was not a "moon," having once been a planet or planetoid.

How had it become a captive of our earth? The answer: the Xenos had engineered the extraordinary feat without too much difficulty.

The event was not a complete surprise to the world's astronomers. Early in December of 1996, astronomers who were checking the upcoming opposition of the asteroid *Eros* were unable to locate it in its customary orbit.*

Eros, one of the major asteroids, belongs to a group of huge fragments that once constituted the fifth planet of the solar system, orbiting between Mars and Jupiter. What caused this former world to explode or disintegrate, we do not know.

Today, its former orbit swarms with millions of planetary fragments, some very small, others huge and irregular chunks, called the asteroids.

Eros, because of its eccentric orbit, came closer to the earth than any other heavenly body, with the exception of the moon. Every 845-1/2 days, or two years and three weeks, it approached at times within 14 million miles of the earth.

When astronomers failed to find it in its customary orbit, they checked with the world's most efficient observatory located in the American sector of the moon. Even they could not find the missing planetoid.

Then, during the last week in December, a terrestrial *spacesweeper patrol*** four million miles out suddenly

*Eros was discovered on August 13, 1898, by Dr. G. Witt at the Urania Observatory, Berlin, Germany. It is known as number 433 asteroid.

**Spacesweeper Patrols* clear space of meteorites and other solid fragments that could cause collisions with spaceships. Some 60 *cosmatomic spacesweepers* continuously patrol all space from Mercury to Mars. The spacesweepers long ago atomized all space-wrecks. They located them by radar and then volatilized the object by *cosmatomic* blasts. During the past few years, the spacesweepers concentrated on the big periodic meteoric showers, such as the Perseids, Leonids, Orionids and Germinids. According to the WSA (World Spacesweep Authority), these have now been completely disintegrated into microscopical dust—no longer a menace to interplanetary travel.

solved the riddle.

Twenty huge 10-Balls were "towing" a large mass, about 15 miles long, toward the earth!

Captain George Wiltz, of the spacesweeper, stated in his radio report that if the Xenos maintained the same speed, they should reach the vicinity of the earth around January 9 or 10.

The forecast proved accurate. The Xenos, as we have seen, placed Eros—for this it proved to be—in an earth orbit on January 10.

Its slightly elliptical orbit is about 790 miles above the earth. It revolves around us in 99-1/8 minutes; *hence we see it rise and set almost fourteen times every day.*

The actual dimensions of brick shaped Eros are a little over fourteen miles long and five miles thick on the average. Like Luna—our old moon—it always presents the same side to us. As Eros is only 790 miles distant from the earth, its seventy-square-mile surface reflects the sunlight strongly and its proximity makes it look as big as the much larger moon, which is actually 238,000 miles away from us.

The new moon naturally aroused tremendous excitement among the world's population. Dozens of questions were asked that no one could answer immediately.

What were the Xenos up to *now?* Did this, their latest exploit, not prove that they were here to stay? Was the new moon another space station that dwarfed all human-built ones? Would Eros not make it much easier to attack us in the future? There were many other sinister speculations, but as so often happens when humanity is presented with a major new phenomenon, none of the guesses proved correct.

During the months to come, a number of human expeditions landed on Eros. They were not molested by the Xenos, who paid no attention to them as long as they did not come closer than a mile from the center of the planetoid, where huge excavations apparently were in progress.

To observers equipped with optical equipment, it seemed that a number of vast shafts were being blasted, large enough to act as "hangars" for the outsize 10-Balls. Indeed, several of these machines were seen in the process of disappearing below the surface of the asteroid. What were they doing inside this little world? The answer, never guessed by anyone, came only later.

In the meantime, the humans explored practically the entire surface of the new moon, both above and below, as well as the rough sides. Even without opposition, this was not easy, because on such a tiny world, the average human weighs only one tenth of an ounce. If anyone jumped up into space, he would never come back but would keep going in a new orbit around the earth.

How, then, did one walk on such a precarious would? The best way it was found was by roping together all explorers, and anchoring one end of the rope either to the spaceship or to Eros. The alternative was to attach powerful magnetic plates to the underside of the explorer's shoes. This method worked on Eros because the asteroid was composed mainly of nickel-iron, interspersed with granite-like material. If the explorer watched where he stepped, he could usually see where there was iron, so the task was not impossible.

Naturally, all the men had to don space suits before they left their spacecraft, for there was absolutely no air on Eros.

Because there were fourteen Eros "days" to one earth day, each "day" on the planetoid had fifty minutes sunlight and fifty minutes darkness. Hence, earth men had to be equipped with a portable electric light to find their way around during the fifty minutes night in the earth's shadow.

The explorers usually went back to their spaceship during the short fifty minutes night. When sunlight broke through once more, they flew to a new location on Eros with their spaceship and then left the ship for further exploring.

As far as was ascertained at the time, no 10-Balls stationed on earth ascended to Eros. It seemed therefore that a distinct and separate task force had been assigned to the much larger 10-Balls which "captured" Eros and put it into orbit over the earth. The same force was apparently doing the new construction work on the asteroid, too. How long that work would take and *what* the mysterious work actually was remained anyone's guess for many months.

9

SPACE

METROPOLIS

Duke Dubois and Donny, as had been their habit B.I.—Before Invasion—were listening to music in the spacious living room of their villa one Sunday night. Of late, the Xeno occupation had left them little leisure time, but tonight there was a welcome lull.

But it wasn't to be. As Duke strode across the room to turn on another Biomusic recording, his private visiphone came on, red signal flashing.

Duke's assistant from the Science Council room was on the *visiscreen.*

"Dr. Dubois," said Manternach, "we have just learned that the large 10-Ball machines doing the mysterious construction work on Eros have left in the direction of the Moon. Your instructions were to inform you immediately should such an eventuality occur.

"As per plan, I have alerted *Columbia Spacefield* to ready our new cosmatomic spaceship. I also called up Drs. Barrens, Fielding and Brackenridge. Four *cosmipropelled spacesuits* are ready, too, at the field. What are your instructions now?"

"Excellent," said Dubois. "I'll be at the field in thirty minutes. Tell my associates to meet me there for immediate takeoff."

"That's the one chance we have been waiting for," Dubois said hurriedly to Donny. "Now I hope we will find out what the Xenos are really up to. I only hope it will give us sufficient time to reconnoiter before the construction team gets back."

"But," observed Donny, "how do you know they didn't leave guards?"

"Impossible," said Duke. "We know the work hasn't progressed sufficiently to leave anyone behind for days. That would mean air locks, air supply, food, water and a hundred other things. Besides, so far they have never molested our people as long as we didn't come too close to the excavations. One man did and he became electrically charged so strongly that long sparks started to come out of his magnetized shoes. He beat a hasty retreat. No, dear, we are in no danger—we have good instruments, too, that warn us should there be a force-field or other electrical barrier. I am sure we will be back in twelve hours or less."

He kissed Donny goodbye, ascended to his private flight room at the top of the villa, where he donned his cosmiflyer gear. He then opened the door to the terrace, stepped out and was immediately airborne. He took a northwest course after he had ascended five hundred feet. As it was late at night, he had turned on the red and green lights on his shoulder rack before he left his house.

In a few minutes he passed Number 12 *airofficer* at the 1,000 foot "single-flyer" traffic level, signaled twice with his yellow *headbeacon,* received the two green "go ahead" flashes and turned north to the Columbia Spacefield, which he had already spotted. He turned on his radiophone, energized with electronoptic waves, gave his serial number, and announced to the *electron-tower* at the field that he would arrive in ten minutes. Landing permission was given at once by the tower. He descended into the invisible electronic glide beam and was soon in the midst of his associates, who had preceded him.

The space flyer was ready and waiting with experienced pilot Frank Vianden at the controls. He had already made four trips to Eros since it was placed into its new orbit by the Xenos and he assured the four scientists that there was nothing to the short trip.

Everybody strapped himself into his seat and in seconds they were off. They were not to don their cosmipropelled space suits until they were ready to land on Eros. The pilot studied his charts while they were accelerating gradually, straight up.

In the olden days of space flight, there was always the bothersome problem of heat from air-friction as a spaceship had to traverse the atmosphere at high speed. This meant weighty machinery for the near zero degree Fahrenheit cabin temperature compensation required when the outside of the ship glowed dull red. Even so, many pioneers died when the heat inside the cabin went over 600 degrees.

Nowadays, of course, there is no such problem. We fly the 100 miles of the earth's densest atmospheric blanket at a leisurely speed of 750 miles an hour and are above the main air body in 30 or 40 minutes. Once 200 miles up, the pilot sets his course. Now he can accelerate as fast as he desires, as there is no air to heat up the ship.

Naturally, without the cosmatomic power supply, this could never have been accomplished—in the old days, the fuel supply for the rocket propulsion took nearly 95 percent of the space and weight. Today, a small ship like the six-passenger *Steller-408*, which carried the five-man Eros expedition, required a weight of only 22 pounds of *atofuel*. That took up only 1-1/2 cubic feet of space, including the heavy lead shielding.

Cosmatomic rockets, used only for the duration of the ship's main acceleration, give out an incandescent steam of particles. During such time, a special type of sand is disintegrated, which gives the desired acceleration. Once the ship has reached its maximum speed in space, say 25,000 miles an hour, no further sand is used. Not more than 300 pounds of sand are carried on the average moon trip. The pilot switches over to *electronwind* once he has overcome the earth's gravitation. Then pure cosmatomic power is used.

If the ship is only orbiting around the earth, no power of any kind is used, except for correcting blasts during the redirection maneuvers of the flight, landing operations, slowing down and so forth.

To make the trip to Eros, the Stellar-408 had to ascend first to a point near the orbit of Eros some 800 miles above the Earth. Then the ship was accelerated until it reached a speed nearly equal that of Eros—18,000 miles an hour.

They were now moving from west to east on account of the retrograde motion of the little moon.

Soon Eros hove into sight a few miles above them, passing them slowly. Pilot Vianden gave the ship a few short power blasts and in several minutes they were flying above Eros at exactly the same speed.

Vianden then switched to electronwind power and in

seconds the ship landed on the earth's second largest moon. He next turned on the ship's bottom electromagnet, which anchored it safely to the asteroid's surface.

The four scientists, who were now in their cosmipropelled spacesuits, entered the ship's air lock. In less than another minute, they were out in the open. Two men went to the right side of the Stellar-408, two to the left. They carefully held on to the safety handgrips bolted all around the ship. These grips were vital, for each man now weighed less than 2-1/2 ounces on Eros despite his bulky, self-propelled spacesuit.

There are two kinds of the Dubois one-man flying suits: one, the *cosmiflyer,* is for terrestrial use only. The *cosmipropelled spacesuit* is used in the vacuum of space.

The earth type does not need an airtight suit, the second one does. In addition, the latter must have the usual plastic space head-globe.

With the cosmic-energy-propelled spacesuit, men can fly around *outside* their spaceships to make repairs and propel themselves in any direction without fear of getting lost in space, as long as they stay near their ship.

At a signal of the pilot, who now had switched off the holding magnet, the four men lifted the ship clear and walked it toward the excavations a mile away. This caused them no effort at all because of the minute gravity of Eros—their spaceship now weighed only a few pounds. All four men had to wear magnetic soles on their shoes; without them they could not have walked at all without being propelled upward. The least muscular effort with their unanchored feet would have sent them flying into space. In that case, they would have had to turn on their cosmipropelled rockets to get back.

In a few minutes they had walked the ship to within one hundred yards of the excavation. Here they put the Stellar-

408 down and the pilot immediately secured it magnetically to the nickel-iron surface of Eros.

The four scientists now unfastened the detection instrument box—which was about the size of a typewriter case—from an indentation on the ship. They switched it on and a green light appeared. If there had been any type of radiation, a red light would have gone on. Dubois himself strapped the case to his chest, where he could watch the lights and several meters.

Now the pilot instructed the men to attach themselves to their safety lines. These were four thin, but very strong wires, which the men fastened around their waists. If anything went wrong, the pilot could also converse with all over the radio phone.

In a few minutes, Dubois and his associates had walked to the rim of the first, and the largest, excavation. As they had guessed, no Xenos were in sight. The instrument case's light was still green.

They looked in stupefaction at the huge hole, 300 feet or more across. In the glaring, hot sunlight they could see it went down at least 500 feet, maybe more.

"Has anyone ever seen such an immense, perfectly round hole in all his life?" shouted Dubois over the phone. "Look at the wall, glass-smooth, as if the entire inner surface had been polished to a mirror finish! Who said 'excavation'—this hole must have been volatilized with temperatures of over 25,000° Fahrenheit, and more!

"I propose we go down one at a time. I'll go first. Because I weigh only a few ounces, I'll just jump—the momentum will make me go down. I can always use my cosmirockets to brake my fall. Barnes, please disconnect my safety wire from you. Here I go!"

In about fifteen minutes, he shouted excitedly, "Come down, all of you—no use frying in that torrid sunlight. No human has ever seen a sight like this! Just jump, the low gravity makes you come down slowly. My distance-radar reads 760 feet down."

The three other scientists went down together but separated by fifteen to twenty feet along the rim of the hole so they could not become entangled in each other's life wires.

The sight that met their unbelieving eyes, once they turned their powerful *electronight* torches on the scene, was overpowering.

The Xenos were building a vast metropolis inside of Eros.

The term "building" did not express the project correctly. The whole sub-stratum city—one can't say underground—was burned or molten from Eros itself. And it was composed entirely of nickel-iron and black granite.

There was a huge dome covering the city in all directions as far as the scientists' powerful torches could reach. This unbelievably large concave ceiling-dome was fully one hundred feet above the highest structure. It was smooth and highly polished, the nickel-iron surface glistening like burnished chrome.

The dwellings were all like apartment house blocks—yet all were in a single piece, fashioned in some way from Eros itself. Nothing seemed to have been "built," but rather heat-blasted or volatilized from the mother metal-rock.

All the huge apartment "houses" were hexagonal in shape. All rooms were hexagonal, too.

"Just like a bee honeycomb," said Dubois, after he could finally speak again. "*Now* I am convinced we have to do with an insect-like race!"

A quick calculation by one of the men showed that each apartment house block had about 1,500 hexagonal rooms. All rooms were of the same size, about twelve feet in the largest dimension, but only eight feet high. None of the apartments had windows of any kind. Inside, the huge containing walls had ramps that ascended from the street floor to the top storey. These ramps were about six feet wide, connecting with all the corridors of the building. There were no stairs in evidence anywhere.

The scientists noted all sorts of vertical conduit holes or ducts in the "comb" part, where the walls of the rooms met, undoubtedly for plumbing, wires or other communications, heating and cooling devices, to be installed later.

There seemed to be no "bathrooms" or "kitchens" so far. But as each apartment had four "rooms," perhaps bathrooms and kitchen were assigned to one room, for later interior construction, if indeed the Xenos used such things.

Elevators seemed not to be provided. Evidently these—if there were to be any—would be *outside* the house block.

Dr. Brackenridge, one of the scientists, who, unfortunately, had a vast vacuum in lieu of imagination, constantly kept criticizing the various Xeno architectural innovations for the want of certain—to him—obvious arrangements. Finally Dubois became so irritated that he shut him off with:

"Brack, you know what my father used to say? *'Never show a fool an unfinished house!'* "

What struck the scientists most was what one of them termed "the unholy cleanliness" and order, in a city only 20 percent finished. There were no debris, no dust, no disorder of any kind. Every building glittered and sparkled with a high finish.

Every one of the men wrote notes furiously, so that they could make a full report later of the indescribable wonders of this new metropolis-in-the-sky.

At one point they came upon an arresting apartment

block, obviously a sample for all others. On the mirror-smooth stark outside walls a Xeno artist-decorator had heat-engraved in bas relief the most beautifully haunting esoteric designs ever seen.

These designs, the scientists thought, gave a pictorial representation of life itself—primeval animal cells, the source from which all life springs. There were hundreds of these designs, all of breathtaking beauty, all different, all probably representing actual sub-electron microscopic views of the most minute life-cells. Of course these were heroic size designs, each six to eight feet across—enlarged many million times from the originals.

The designs seemed to move and scintillate under the powerful torch lights. Sensing something unusual, Dubois suddenly shouted:

"Lights out!"

Now in total darkness, the figures miraculously came to life. They moved, or one had the illusion of motion—the life-cells seemed to vibrate in breathtakingly delicate undulations, scintillating here, then there, the multicolors coruscating continuously, weaving in and out.

"What a terrific spectacle!" cried Dubois. "Evidently the bas relief lines are filled with a variety of radioactive luminous elements. What an idea!"

Dubois approached the building, but when he came to within twenty feet of it his instrument box suddenly indicated radiation by its red light. He went back and for twenty minutes the men of science silently feasted their eyes on the strange phenomenon of a monument dedicated to the beginning of life itself. They left in awe.

Before departing, after a six-hour stay in *Eros-City,* as they already had dubbed it, the four men made an estimate of the number of Xeno inhabitants it could accommodate. They came to the conclusion that the new city easily could hold from 400,000 to 600,000 Xenos. Many more could be accommodated no doubt—the construction had only begun. Even one million inhabitants would not be too high a figure—there was an abundance of room on, or, rather *in* Eros.

The expedition's return to earth was wholly uneventful. In spite of their remarkable discovery, there was little talk—every one of the scientists was absorbed making notes while the impression of the miraculous city was fresh.

Said Dubois, "It will take a month to digest and record all we have seen—and we'll only then begin the long task of guessing why the Xenos have come here, and what it portends for the earth's future."

10

DEFECTIVE

HUMANITY

With the Xeno invasion in its eighth month, the earth's population was thrown into a frenzy when Dr. Dubois and his associates released their first news report, shortly after their return to earth from our second moon, Eros.

This report gave only a preliminary outline on the "Space Metropolis" now being constructed by the invaders on the earth's newest moon. A voluminous report was to be issued in another month. The news report was careful to state that the construction was only about 20 percent completed, but this was sufficient for the masses, now jittery the world over.

When Eros first swam into view in the sky, the uncomprehending people of the world momentarily were struck dumb with surprise at the new astronomical wonder.

They were not too concerned, however, because they did not at once divine its true significance. Everyone dismissed the new moon as a space station of some sort.

Columnists and science writers everywhere speculated that Eros, being in an almost perfect vacuum, was also thought to be an excellent astronomical space-platform for better communication with the Xenos' "home" base—wherever it was. Amateur scientists were quick to point out that the earth's atmosphere was unsuited for best communication and signaling, but that Eros was an ideal location. Hence the whole world had been lulled into the false belief that the new secondary moon was just another harmless gadget of the invaders.

Then the cold and unnerving realization suddenly burst upon humanity that everything now pointed to a *permanent* occupation by the Xenos, and the masses could restrain themselves no longer.

The "Xenos' City in the Sky," only a short distance above the earth, was now seen as a perpetual threat, from which the invader's will could be directed to enforce any of his demands on the world. The masses were certain that the real Xeno master plan now was to exploit humanity in earnest.

Severe rioting broke out spontaneously all over the planet, taking the various governments completely by surprise. Nothing remotely as intense as these uprisings had been anticipated by any authorities, who frankly did not know how to cope with it.

The mobs looted every imaginable establishment in their delusion that "we might as well get what we can before the Xenos do." Most work was stopped—in some countries for weeks. Reason, it seems, had completely left everyone, even professional thinkers.

This reaction was in reality a long deferred savage

outburst against the Xenos. Because for eight months the more or less aloof invaders had not molested humanity unduly, the world had accepted them with great tolerance and forebearance. After all, they were known to be on a scientific expedition of discovery like that which humans go on.

But such an expedition must be purely temporary in nature; certainly so enlightened a race as the Xenos seemed to be would under no circumstances enslave the earth permanently. That had been the intuitive reasoning of the entire population.

Were not the Xenos sending water from the earth to their own home? Did they not send via radio a rare radioactive element, too? Then why stay on or near the earth?

According to the new reasoning, the water and radioactive element must be fuel to enable a mass immigration to our planet. Hadn't the paplast press warned of this right along?

The population, too, knew from many science reports that there could not be more than 50,000 Xenos on earth and on the moon. *But now Dubois had reported that they were building housing for 600,000 to a million superminds!* No wonder despair and panic gripped the world.

Suddenly, during this upheaval, as is so often true of mob psychology, the rioters found their tongues and became lucidly vocal in expressing their true sentiments:

"We're just dull insects, doing the bidding of superminds." "We are trained fleas—what's the sense of living for the masters?" "They already have trained our children to work for them—we've lost them, too."

These cries of despair spoke of all hope gone. These and similar sayings appeared almost simultaneously all over the world, and were so reported.

Added to these outbreaks were long-dormant, pent-up

demonstrations against The Big-5, "who only talk us to death, but never do anything to get rid of the invaders." "Why don't our stupid scientists invent means to oust the invader?" people asked. "Have our clever scientists sold out to the Xenos, too?"

Psychologists also reasoned that what added fuel to the mental flames was an unreasoning instinct and fear of the completely unidentified and unknown invader. *No one had ever seen a Xeno.*

Here was a mysterious super-entity, so far ahead of man's puny mentality that he could pull every imaginable, invisible string, robbing humans of their 15-million-year-old heritage and birthright.

All these and many similar sentiments, curiously enough, were printed in the world's press because by this time the press, too, had become infected with despair and mob psychology.

For weeks there had not been evolved a single logical counter suggestion that things were not as bad as they appeared.

Indeed, as history was advancing swiftly, the future was to record once more that, as in so many past human upheavals, the infuriated mobs' instincts had a good deal of prescience.

What finally restored a semblance of order was the Dubois report, written in conjunction with over 160 associated world-renowned scientists. This was during March, 1997, the ninth month of the invasion.

Dubois' lengthy report, broadcast to the entire world, was listened to respectfully, as a port of last hope.

We are giving here only the highlights of an hour-and-a-half long talk.

* * *

Most important, as a soothing remedy to a jittery world,

was Dubois' cold, scientific reasoning that there was absolutely nothing in the eight-months'-long Xeno invasion record that showed the slightest evidence that the invaders had designs of any kind on the human welfare, its institutions, its livelihood and its progress.

"On the contrary," said Dubois, "my colleagues and I are astonished to see how infinitely little they have really interfered. Have humans in their entire history shown such consideration in *their* invasions? Only a few hundred years ago, we practically exterminated the civilization of the Aztecs, the Incas, and, later, the American Indians, to mention just a few. And aren't we behaving very much in the same manner on the moon, which we are now colonizing, fortunately without any lunar population to contend with?

"Let us now give our attention to Eros, which has caused so much unhappiness lately on earth.

"Let us look at the facts as they really are. First, Eros does not belong to the earth. It is only a large rock towed by the Xenos into a new orbit, which happens to be around the earth.

"Why should this fact excite us so mightily? Aren't the Xenos right *on* earth this very minute, nearly 800 miles closer to us than they would be on Eros? If they haven't molested us since they have been here, why should they from Eros? It just doesn't make sense.

"One more point: we scientists have mentioned before the now certain fact that the Xenos have never walked the earth, not because they don't want to—*they cannot do it physically*.

"We have long reasoned that they are certain to come from a small planet where the gravity is very low. They *must* stay in their gravity-conditioned 10-Balls—or go elsewhere. If they descended and tried to walk among us, their unaccustomed new weight would crush them—they would collapse like soft putty under a load.

"And that is, in our opinion, the reason why they captured Eros. As our own exploration has shown, a 150-pound human on Eros weighs only 1/10 ounce—making it an ideal home for the Xenos.

"Moreover, how do we know they *want* to stay in the present orbit around the earth permanently? If they can move the little world out of its original orbit, they can move it to any place in the universe.

"We can think of a lot of better places in the universe than a miniature planetoid orbiting around the earth!

"We are convinced that the Xenos are *not* staying permanently near the earth, even though Eros may be a permanent home and vehicle for them.

"Indeed, our thinking is that the little planetoid is nothing but a glorified Space Cruise-Ship! Eros is now being fitted out to become a self-contained world that may go anywhere in our universe for research. We shall give you our reasons for this conclusion shortly.

"The miniature planet could go into a very much better orbit somewhere between Venus and the earth. Here there would be more sunlight—if they needed it.

"And the solar system is only one of billions. If they have the necessary time, there is no reason why they cannot select the system that suits them best.

"It seems to us that they are building so many dwellings in Eros only because they expect to maintain a large population for thousands of years to come, *during which time they will visit uncountable worlds*. During such voyages, the entire present population and many future generations will have died and been replaced by newborn ones.

"Why do we reason thus? Our recent Eros exploration,

short as it was, has convinced us that it is being fitted out for such a purpose. We cite here only a few items from our findings:

"An immense water reservoir had already been fashioned, measuring over one mile long by about one-half mile deep. This is far more water than the ten times larger city of New York could use in a year.

"A very shallow tank over two miles long, but only a few feet deep, most likely for growing some form of protein, like algae or chlorella and possibly some forms of mushrooms.

"Directly adjoining the metropolis we found an entirely separate city, which, judging from the various buildings of every type and shape, will become the 'industrial' plant or workshops. Here evidently anything and everything that will ever be required will be fashioned.

"Vast hangars for the 10-Balls have already been melted and volatilized from the nickel-iron-granite, which soon will be equipped complete with air locks.

"The entire metropolis will have air locks, too, to maintain the Xenos' interior atmosphere at low pressure. We have calculated from various data that this atmosphere will be only one-fourth as dense as the terrestrial air. Exactly what its composition will be in terms of gas content, we do not know as yet.

"What becomes of the huge quantities of nickel-iron-granite that have been excavated, or, rather, melted? It is being remelted to form housing, shops and other structures. Not all of it has been reused so far, as huge mounds on the surface of Eros testify.

"During its space roaming through the universe, *everything* in the little planetoid must be completely regenerated all the time. Nothing can ever be discarded—one cannot 'throw away' material or acquire new supplies during uninterrupted space voyages.

"Whatever is 'used up' is reused in another form. Air is completely renewed chemically, continuously. Human—and animal—waste is also continually reworked into its chemical constituents.

"Nothing of any kind is destroyed—it all stays on or in the small world, to be used over and over in a never-ending cycle.

"What is the philosophy and purpose of all this? Once a civilization has reached the, to us, fantastic heights that the Xenos have, the mind is no longer satisfied with the humdrum existence on a small world. The mind and body take wing into the unexplored mysteries of the universe, because here, and here only, can a far-advanced intelligence meet nature on a level that can still awe it.

"Intelligence, whether human or Xenian, is never long satisfied with what it has learned to know—the magnet of the great unknown is forever attracting it to new wonders, and once those near at hand are completely explored, new and greater ones are to be found only in the deep recesses of space.

"Nature has fashioned these ultra wonders for countless billions of years, while even the oldest living intelligence-endowed beings have existed for only a few short minutes on a comparative scale. Hence no intelligence can ever hope to catch up with nature's continuing creations.

"It would seem to us scientists that from these vistas the idea of the Xenos orbiting dizzily around our puny earth forever—or even a few years—is ludicrous in the extreme."

In retrospect, it appears that Dr. Dubois' talk did much to reassure the masses once more. In any event, the world furor died down quickly and did not rear its ugly face again.

11

INTELLECTUAL

EXPLOSION

During the tenth month of the Xenian invasion it became apparent that humanity was undergoing the most fundamental change in its long history.

It will be recalled that, five months earlier, the Xenos had descended on all of the world's schools. Under deep hypnosis, the children, ages six to eight, had received two skull punctures in the region of the frontal lobe. All children were unconscious for six hours, during which period the Xenos had planted certain biological cells in the front part of the brain. These grafts, it was ascertained later, quickly grew into two large, bean-sized new organs.

Five months later, these glands had completely matured, although they had not increased in size. The grafting technique of the Xeno scientists had been so astounding that 98 out of 100 grafts were completely successful. No child under six or over eight had been treated; the Xenos evidently had their own means of determining which of the children should be chosen. Final school statistics showed that fewer than 80 percent of all "abducted" children were "punctured." Evidently the Xenos, during the deep hypnosis of the youngsters, instituted a series of tests to select only those individuals shown to be completely fit.

That they knew exactly what they were about was subsequently proven indubitably. The rejected children all had subnormal mental—or physical—development. They were defective in all cases because of impaired heredity factors.

The final statistics indicated that almost 188 million children had been successfully treated out of a total of almost 6 billion of the world's population.

Originally, a panel of fifty-nine of the foremost geneticists and biologists had ventured the opinion that a fair percentage of the treated children would transmit their new glands to succeeding generations. Their feeling was based on an unproven hunch that the Xenos knew far more about cytology than human scientists.

As it turned out, they underestimated the superminds completely.

For the Xenos had made certain that practically all "grafted" children would hand down the new organs to their descendants.

Here was a far-reaching innovation in *"accelerated heredity,"* as it is now known, never experienced before in the annals of science on such a vast scale.

It was the famed Dr. Armand Winterthur, the world's greatest living biologist, who was the first scientist to call attention to the fact that the Xenos, besides implanting new gland grafts in the children's brains, had also simultaneously altered certain genes in their reproductive cells.

He professed not to know what method the Xenos used in locating the correct genes and then influencing them so they would be certain to transmit the new heredity factors, *but actually he had incontrovertible proof.*

During the preceding month, Dr. Winterthur had photographed over twelve hundred germ cells of treated children of both sexes. This he accomplished with his recently perfected *transmicroluminator*. This instrument uses an atomic flash-ray lamp that gives over 10 million candlepower. The exposure lasts only 1/500 second, thus creating no burns. The light is so powerful that it goes right through the densest part of the body, as do X rays, but unlike the latter, it gives a microphotograph perfect in every detail, not just shadows.

The subject to be examined lies over a very sensitive photographic film on a special table. A technician now makes several *visual* shots with the transmicroluminator, to obtain an exact focus on the genes he wishes to photograph. No picture is taken during this test. Next he focuses the instrument, which automatically brings the film into focus, too. He presses a button and the photomicro-picture is made.

In the twelve hundred pictures that Professor Winterthur took of the "new" children, there could be no question that genes had been altered. Even a non-expert could see the difference between treated and untreated genes.

Comparative pictures taken of the non-treated children showed the unaltered genes clearly and conclusively. Thus there seemed little doubt that all gland-grafted children would transmit the Xeno-induced heritage to their future offspring.

To say that the *Xenofied* children—as they soon became known—averaging seven years of age, caused a major sociological revolution is a fantastic understatement. It is almost impossible to describe their worldwide impact on humanity.

Picture, if you can, the devastating onslaught of tens of millions of seven-year-old Newtons, Einsteins, Mozarts, Archimedes'—and other giants among great scientists, statesmen, mathematicians, essayists and philosophers—and you will obtain an approximate understanding of history's greatest intellectual explosion.

Seven-year-olds, fully matured mentally, holding their own with the foremost minds alive—and usually surpassing them in every direction. Indeed, there was no field in which they were not masters—and this only five months after acquiring their new super-organs.

Not only were they the most voracious readers ever seen—they were also the fastest. Almost without exception they had perfect photographic memories, a gift rarely seen before the superchildren arrived.

Teams of middle-aged educational giants watched in amazement a score of seven-year-olds leafing leisurely through volumes of encyclopaedias at the average rate of 2-1/2 hours per volume—then reciting on demand any article verbatim, or sketching out, in complete detail, any of the illustrations.

While photographic memories are a wondrous gift, few such exceptional minds in the past could derive the full benefit from their talent. Recalling thousands of facts and figures is a very impressive feat, but putting them to intelligent use is quite another thing.

There have, for instance, always been great musicians who could, on demand, play hundreds, even thousands of musical selections. But few were like the child Mozart who was a phenomenal composer to boot.

The Xenofied children—practically all of them—were masters in their chosen fields. It was breathtaking to see a mathematician, just turned eight, best several gray-haired professors of higher mathematics on intricate problems and theorems.

These super-intelligent children excelled as logicians as well—and what is more important, they applied their knowledge into practical channels. As if this were not sufficient, they were exceedingly aggressive and could hold their own in almost every debate.

Naturally, their schools were none too happy with this state of affairs, as no teacher could keep up with them. Even when transferred to higher grades, they quickly upset any normal routine and proved a detriment to non-processed children.

As a rule, they went to universities or other seats of higher learning—if there was room for them—but even here, far too often, *they* instructed the instructors.

They had, of course, to be guided in all manual accomplishments, such as writing, typing, drafting and in all the arts and sciences that required physical dexterity. Yet even here they learned with extraordinary rapidity.

Soon the world was confronted with a problem of great magnitude. What to do with these 188 millions of children who had completely outgrown all schools and seats of learning? Manifestly, their immature childish bodies could not be allowed to do the work of mature men. There were, fortunately, antichild labor laws in all civilized countries the world over, to stop such abuse if it had been attempted.

A partial solution was tried out, and so far this proved fairly satisfactory in many countries. In the mornings, children, accompanied by state guardians, were taken to various points of interest, to courts in session, to libraries, to museums, on various sightseeing trips, and so forth.

Once a month, they were taken to other cities away from home on similar missions. In the afternoon, they went for a few hours to the country's great industrial plants. Here they viewed various processes or manufacturing operations. At the end of the visit, they became paid consultants for one hour. Their opinions on various processes and possible improvements were solicited and it was surprising how helpful and original many of their ideas and solutions were. The factories and commercial institutions paid the young consultants well for their advice, and the fees were equally distributed over the entire "class." The money was always banked and could not be touched until the youths reached sixteen—in some countries, eighteen.

While the Xenofied children tended to associate themselves, naturally enough, with their own kind, they did not deliberately shun other children, nor were they snobbish because of the others' much lower mentality. They nearly always were patient, trying to explain and impart knowledge to the less fortunate youngsters. Nor did they think themselves abnormal or especially gifted—no more than the occasional wonder children did in past ages.

It was the parents of the wonder children who took the brunt of the biological revolution, and their lot was not a happy one. Since this was not a new phenomenon on earth, parents of other ages had had the same problems, except that then many parents exploited the gifts of their genius offspring shamefully. Also, there were not too many such children then.

Now, suddenly there were 376 million parents who were aghast at the super-abilities of their children, and, worse, who could not cope with them.

Practically all grownups were hopelessly behind in

mentality, compared to that of their "young geniuses."
Most of the time they had no idea what the child was
talking about. He might as well have spoken a foreign
language. Where there were two gifted youngsters in one
family, the situation was naturally much worse for the
elders.

The galling thing was that the children, even from the
beginning, ran the household far more than children ever
did in the past. The youngsters mixed in *all* the affairs of
their elders, from their father's business to his finances.
Mothers were taught the ABC's of running the home to
getting the most out of their household allowances.

The youngsters originated their own inventions and
labor-saving gadgets. They put their elders to work on
various money-making schemes that usually took care of
their spare time and proved successful in most cases.

They taught them logic and improved their health in
many ways. As walking encyclopedias, they were never
stumped on any topic, and, better yet, they knew always
how to apply their knowledge in a practical manner.

The conditions related above were naturally not universal
in all homes. For there was a fair percentage of gifted
parents, too. Yet even they had to bow to the superior
knowledge of their super-offspring in all too many
instances. It was usually the fresh approach and the
devastating logic of the brilliant youngster that defeated the
older minds.

What was most humiliating to most parents, however,
was the children's extraordinary fund of sexological
science. It was always disconcerting to adults to listen to a
biological sex lecture, given in a factual manner, as if the
child was teaching them how to create a new hybrid flower.

Since the children had read every important sexological
volume and memorized all sexo-medical magazines and

periodicals, it was invariably the parents who were embarrassed, never their offspring.

If there were more than three or four children in the family, the parents were certain to be lectured on simple birth-spacing, so the mother would not be burdened with another early arrival. Some of the Xenofied seven-year-olds could become quite rabid on that subject. And, as a rule, the parents listened to the youngster's logic.

If their elders were surly and not happy sexually, the telepathic child would soon know why. He—or she as the case might be—would induce the father to read a marked copy of a book on sex technique. Then the youngster would instruct the mother similarly, pointing out to her that it was better to satisfy her husband, lest he look for greener pastures.

If this seems unrealistic to the older generation who had never been exposed to Xenofied seven-year-olds, let them realize that the inexperienced child, who, of course, could not very well know the intimate routine of intercourse, nevertheless knew its mechanics.

A seven-year-old child is never sexually embarrassed, for the simple reason that he has never experienced deep sexual emotion. That would come later. In the meanwhile, the child looks upon the idea of the mating act as a purely mechanical one.

A good parallel for sexually embarrassed parents comes to mind: Give an average—not the genius type—child his first electric motor and battery. The motor's rotor spins fast, sparks at the contacts and educates the youngster.

He does not have to know that the battery's electrons create a magnetic field in the motor (emotion in man), that the electric current is translated into kinetic energy and motion in the motor (life force in man)—plus a number of other physical phenomena that occur simultaneously in the motor—and in man, too.

Thus most precocious youngsters can spout learnedly about many things they have never experienced in their own bodies—they are not encumbered by useless mental baggage—yet their fundamental knowledge or understanding often is as good as, or better than their elders'.

This is precisely why parents for countless ages have never been able to differentiate between their own sex-biased emotions and their children's matter-of-fact, uncomplicated, naïve viewpoints.

Parents should take a completely detached view of all sex matters—vis-à-vis their children—as if they were discussing the weather. This would make for a far better and healthier home atmosphere and family relationship.

But there was one subject on which the super children unanimously were firebrands—perhaps revolutionary is the better term.

That subject was fanatic opposition to war. They not only talked about it continuously, but they took steps to spread their gospel in every land of the globe.

Whenever they had a chance, they wangled their way, never alone but always in groups, into the great communication centers where they appeared on the radio, television, and even occasionally on the sacrosanct, all-penetrating, cosmivoice, when they had an especially momentous message for the population.

Their anti-war propaganda was always so lucid, so convincing and so logical that the world's paplast press soon front-paged it as a regular feature. It became clear soon that here was perhaps the greatest concerted effort ever undertaken, not only to outlaw war but to make it impossible to engage in it.

The horrors of nuclear and cosminuclear war, radiation war and all other forms of warfare were drummed into the consciousness of the world without let-up, until all humanity knew, as it had never known before, what atomic and sub-atomic war really meant.

Gifted orators too, the children now regularly penetrated the ruling centers of the world, from the Congress of the United States to the Supreme Soviet of the U.S.S.R., from the Parliament of Great Britain and the National Assembly and Council of the Republic of France to the Diet of Japan and the Supreme Commission of the Sudan.

The rulers of all countries, whether they were presidents, kings, queens, or the Mikado, fell under the hypnotic spell of the new ultra-intellectual generation.

Hypnotic was the correct term—or perhaps Dr. Dubois' definition *metahypnosis* explained the new force better.

Said he in a worldwide multilingual broadcast:

Perhaps you will recall that when our talented friends, the Xenos, first began the dual puncturing of our six- or seven-year-old children, we soon knew that they had grafted two minute new organs on the forebrains of our young. Within weeks, it became all too apparent that the two pea-sized organs had enhanced the intelligence of our children enormously.

We were certain that one of the organs was responsible for the new intellectuality and we theorized that the other was a telepathic organ of some sort.

It now appears that we were only partly correct as to the second.

From several thousand tests conducted by our scientists all over the world, we have ascertained that we have to do with an entirely new biological phenomenon—a super-hypnotic force, which we have termed metahypnotism. Associated with it to a certain extent is telepathy.

Many of my listeners know from their own experience that if our gifted youngsters set their minds or wills to it, they can easily influence us at a distance—particularly when it comes to their fanatic anti-war ideas.

All that is necessary is that they transfix us *once* with their brilliant phosphorescent eyes. Henceforth we are under their spell in various degrees.

Incidentally, the high luminosity of their eyes is not a new biological phenomenon, nor is it a purely nocturnal effect of night beasts of prey. Many humans have it, too—the high phosphorescence can easily be seen during the day, during an individual's hysteria, terror or great stress. Our Xenofied children have it with hardly an exception, and we have learned that the luminosity of their eyes is far more brilliant than that of any other mortals.

After long deliberation, we have come to the inescapable conviction that the metahypnotic-telepathic organ was deliberately implanted by the Xenos for one purpose only—

To breed out war from the predatory human race.

War has been on this planet for countless millions of years. All living beings wage war, from plant life to mammals.

War is an hereditary disease with humans. We can never call ourselves civilized until it is completely bred out of us. We cannot just *think* ourselves out of it—it goes much too deep for that.

The Xeno superminds, who have been watching us for many months, must know all about war, far more than we shall ever know. They must look upon us as a loving parent looks upon a three-year-old playing with matches. Only *our* matches today are nuclear and sub-nuclear ones—and worse.

Hence they applied the only possible remedy—making war so repugnant to us that in succeeding generations we shall look back upon our terrible dark *telegenocide** war age as we look back now on cannibalism and human sacrifices.

And that is the real reason our children were impregnated with their new organs.

We can only hope and pray that our Xeno benefactors have not been too late in guiding human destiny.

*   *   *

It was late April, during the tenth month of the inva-

**Telegenocide (from *tele*-distant, *genos*-race, *cide*-kill) is the systematic extermination of a whole people or nation, from a distance, by nuclear, cosminuclear or similar means.

sion, that a number of new occurrences in Xenian behavior were noted by earth scientists.

Dr. Dubois, as well as all other physicists, had won-
dered how the Xenos and their 10-Balls could be so self-
sustaining during all the months of their earth occupation.

That they could easily survive not only for ten months
but for ten years, or even a hundred years, was well
understood by every scientist. After all, they had very
probably traveled over great astronomical distances to get
to our earth; therefore the problem of life for many years
in a hermetically sealed sphere was no novelty for the
Xenos. As every human knew also by that time, nothing
was ever "discarded" by the invaders, with the exception of
a few pounds of spongy lead pellets, probably cosminuclear
waste.

All other "waste" therefore must have been reprocessed
continuously in a never-ending cycle. Yet up to the tenth
month, earth watches had never seen two 10-Balls come
together or contact each other. Each 10-Ball thus was a
complete entity, functioning independently, yet in unison
with the entire fleet.

But during the last week in April, there was a change
in routine. A radio report from the moon stated that
twelve of the much larger 10-Balls stationed on the moon,
near their lunium mine, had suddenly left in the general
direction of the earth.

Within hours, the fleet of twelve 10-Balls had arrived
on earth and they were soon busy contacting each earth-
stationed 10-Ball.

The "contact" was extremely curious. Each new arrival
stationed itself some three hundred feet from a now im-
mobilized 10-Ball. Then the two machines bent their purple tubes in unison until they formed the letter U. Thus
the two tubes formed a single connecting link between
each other. The machines remained in this position for

less than fifteen minutes.

Then the larger 10-Ball moved to the next earth-stationed one. The whole operation of contacting the entire invading fleet took but a day. After that, the twelve "messenger" 10-Balls took off for the moon again, where only two machines had remained at their lunium mine.

Our scientists immediately guessed that the twelve moon-based machines were a supply fleet *to refuel the earth-based 10-Balls* with new nuclear, or other fuel. Did they bring a supply of lunium to the terrestrial invasion fleet? Or had they reprocessed, or transmuted the lunium into some other element—or was lunium only a necessary adjunct or additive to another high-energy fuel? No one on earth possessed enough knowledge to supply the answer.

In the meantime, earth observers stationed on Eros had reported that the original construction fleet of 10-Balls had never returned from the moon in its original task force.

Only a single large 10-Ball had come to Eros, but according to the observers, its crew worked on the outside of Eros exclusively; there was, as far as could be ascertained, no interior work done at all.

This was easy to deduce because the new 10-Ball arrival worked at a distance of five miles from the huge shaft that led to the interior wonder city, still as unfinished as it was when Dubois and his fellow scientists had inspected it a while back.

During the first week, nothing definite about the construction work on top of Eros could be seen, because the purple tube, widely expanded at the bottom, covered up whatever went on.

During the second week, the 10-Ball moved higher and then observers, several miles distant, noted that the Xeno construction crew had fashioned a huge, perfectly round, iron or steel sphere about five hundred feet in diameter.

A week later another sphere, smaller in diameter, was added, stuck or welded on top of the original one.

Then in quick succession, other spheres, or globes, were added, *each smaller than the previous one.*

By June 5, the twelfth month of the invasion, the huge *sphere-tower,* nearly three-quarters of a mile in height, was completed. It had a total of fourteen globes stacked on top of each other. It was the highest artificial tower ever seen by a human.

On June 6, Dr. Dubois and three of his scientists flew to Eros to examine the new Xeno wonder personally. They approached to within two miles of it, marveling at its elegant construction as they observed every last detail of its breathtaking architecture through their *tele-magnifiers.*

The way it reflected the sunlight made it seem as if the iron or steel tower had been chrome-plated. Or had it been polished to a mirror finish during the welding process? These were idle questions to which there could be no immediate answers.

"If this spherical-pyramid," said Dubois, "had been constructed on earth, it would weigh hundreds of millions of tons, if all the spheres were solid. Even if they were only 25 percent solid, they would still weigh millions of tons. Here on Eros, where the gravitation is minimal, the total weight is only a few tons—yet even so, this is certainly an achievement of a high order. My hat is off once more to the Xenos."

"And what do you make of the pointed spherical cones at the top?" asked Dr. Dabo Domloder.

"That's easy to understand," answered Dr. Dubois. "They have similar pointed cones on their lunar-based 10-Balls. What we see here is, I am certain, a special communication aerial of some sort. In my opinion it is used not only for communication purposes but for the transfer—or reception—of radiated energy.

"As we have seen already, it is likely that the Xenos transmit transmuted radioactive lunium to their home base.

"We suspect that they will soon navigate Eros away from earth into a new exploration voyage to other parts of the universe. As a huge space cruiser it will have to be supplied occasionally with new energy—superfuel of some kind—to keep going on, and return, too, generations later.

"Where is this essential energy, this fuel, to come from? *To put it simply: from space!* Slowly, mankind is awakening to the staggering fact that space abounds with all sorts of energy, which needs only to be tapped.

"If we are not too far from a star, such as our own sun, there is boundless energy—radiant energy that as yet we are too ignorant to tap in large quantities. This radiant solar energy abounds in X rays, ultraviolet, infrared, cosmic and other rays. The Xenos, we may be certain, know how to tap it, *and store it.*

"But far out in space, where the next sun may be from four light years to dozens of light years distant, and a spaceship may be in pitch darkness for years on end—what then?

"That is precisely what this tower—also an energy tower—must be for. We know today that space abounds with energy, too—even pitch dark space, faintly illuminated only by the cold stare of the far distant fixed stars.

"Yet powerful cosmic and super-cosmic radiation exists throughout space. *And, from certain directions, as we know today, cosmic energy is far more powerful than from others.* Our studies have already indicated that this super-cosmic radiation comes from certain novae—exploding stars or galaxies in collision. This is a phenomenon found throughout the Universe, hence no matter where the Xenos travel, there will always be some form of energy on hand to assist their space cruiser in their travels.

"How they collect or tap this energy, we do not know, but some day we will. It is also probable that not very much energy is required while they travel. Remember, in free space, far from other suns or galaxies, there is hardly any gravitational attraction. Hence, once the spaceship has attained its maximum acceleration, very little extra propelling energy is required because the spaceship—Eros in this instance—practically coasts along on its original speed.

"But other sources of energy to run the city inside Eros—power for light, heat and other purposes—are needed constantly. True, the Xenos will have a very large supply of lunium or similar energy source stowed away that will conceivably last for many years, but extra power for steering, maneuvering and accelerating the ship is required from time to time.

"We may be certain that the tower we see here is the answer to that problem. Sufficient energy from space can be attracted by the tower to fulfill all requirements.

"There is the fascinating possibility that this mammoth iron or steel tower probably acts as a huge magnet in attracting radiation from space. Our own earth, as you know, does exactly that, too.

"Dr. Segomes, if you have taken enough telephotograph films of the tower, I suggest we return to earth to make our report on the latest Xeno wonder."

12

DENOUEMENT

Duke and Donny were giving themselves a rare treat—they were lounging in Duke's study. After the frenetic events of the Xeno invasion that started on June 24, 1996, they had seldom had a chance for an intimate tête-à-tête evening—indeed, they had hardly ever been alone or uninterrupted for more than a few minutes.

Duke had been so occupied with his multifarious science duties that took him all over the world—and out of this world—that he had had practically no family life to speak of.

Donny, too, had been drawn into the whirlpool of the vast Xenian invasion, and was kept away from her home for increasing periods.

Recently she had been elected the United States chairman of the "Society of Xenofied Children's Mothers." These harassed mothers, most of whom no longer could cope with, what had become known—not too euphemistically—as "the little intellectual monsters" were at their wits' end.

The mothers had reached the zero point in their self-esteem, self-respect and discipline. They were nonentities vis-à-vis their supermind offspring, and were rapidly disintegrating as mothers and housewives. The situation became so serious that many had to be placed in mental institutions. Others just left home. The fathers were no better off, but at least they could escape to their jobs.

To try and bring a modicum of order into these homes, societies of intellectual women sprang up spontaneously all over the world. They soon found that the harassed mothers needed strong guidance in their domestic affairs, plus reeducation on a high level. This was no sinecure, even for the highly intelligent guides, since it would take years of continuous effort to repair these blasted homes. Nevertheless, the volunteers went at the task with unswerving ardor—they had to succeed in this, one of the greatest challenges ever to confront sociology.

At the moment, Donny, who just had given Duke a capsule report on these activities, was well pleased with her efforts—she knew that for the long pull, her labors would not be in vain.

"Too bad," she confided wistfully, "*we* do not have one of these wizard-youngsters of our own—by the way, whatever do you think did become of *our* child? And do you realize this is Sunday, June 17—one week from the invasion anniversary, when *we* were 'processed' by the Xenos?"

"Well, of all things!" Duke exclaimed. "I certainly did forget. Inexcusable of me—time certainly evaporated dizzily the past year! We have gone through so much, more than humanity ever experienced in a like period—it's really like a fantastic dream.

"Now, as to your question. I can't help feeling depressed when I think of it. There is absolutely no doubt in my mind that the Xeno scientists have successfully brought our child into the world by *ectogenesis*—they rarely make mistakes, as we know only too well. And ours is not the only one. We know that they must have tens of thousands of other captive infants, if we go by all the countless biological punctures which they performed on other couples.

"At this stage, it is pointless to conjecture what will happen to the myriad youngsters. The most plausible answer—I am distressed to tell you—is that the Xenos will take all the children with them to their miracle underground city on Eros. What finally will become of them is anyone's guess. I am so sorry, dear, please—"

Donny was on the verge of tears, as she felt once more the pangs of the frustration of being denied a child. After she composed herself, she spoke tearfully.

"When . . . when do you think the Xenos will take the children—if there *are* any—to . . . to Eros?"

"That is a difficult question to answer, darling. If you listened to my broadcast on Eros last evening, you know that I spoke about their new 3/4-mile high, spherical-pyramid energy tower and its vast scientific aspects.

"Their great city is less than half finished, as far as we can see. Much, *much* more remains to be done, once a full working force returns to Eros.

"As you know, that force is still on the moon at the lunium mine. If I were to make a very rough guess, I would venture that it might take from three to five months to complete their city. Much can happen during that period."

*　　*　　*

The prophecy of his last sentence was to be fulfilled

faster than Duke Dubois had ever imagined possible. Even as he spoke on that memorable evening of Sunday, June 17, 1997, the maelstrom of terrestrial—and spatial history had come to a crucial focus.

Bedlam and pandemonium broke out simultaneously all over the whole earth, as it had never before—even during wartime. Church bells were ringing, radios and television sets shrieked. The nerve-twanging, sonorous and commanding cosmivoice boomed into every abode and recess of humanity, while history-making events tumbled over each other in an incredible profusion.

In Duke Dubois' study, the sudden bedlam was even more unconfined, if that were possible. Four telephones—one with an emergency *stentorspeaker,* in unison with the cosmivoice, bellowed:

"PRE-FLASH*—INVASION OVER—ALL 10-BALLS GONE AT TOP SPEED IN DIRECTION OF MOON."

The echo of this portentous news was still reverberating when one of Dubois' Columbia secretaries, Miss Mary Windber, came on the visiphone in high excitement:

"Dr. Dubois, please fly over fast with Mrs. Dubois. Will meet you near the mall in Central Park. *I am here with your son!* Hurry."

Speechless and completely unnerved by this astounding news, Duke and Donny somehow scrambled into the elevator in their villa and tumbled out on the roof, where, weak and breathless, they managed to get into their cosmiflyer suits. Within minutes they were winging toward New York's Central Park Mall.

They did not fly alone. Evidently dozens of others had received similar news flashes and were heading for New York's famous park.

---

*Pre-Flash—Preliminary News Flash.

Although it was after 2100 (9:00 PM) and dark else-where, the mall and the entire park were brilliantly illuminated, as in full aaylight, by huge overhead *atolumes*.* This innovation was perfected in 1989 by the Danish physicist, Dr. Niels Thorvaldsen. By means of it, entire cities were now illuminated brilliantly from above. The principle is simple. Huge, hollow, double-walled lentil-shaped magnesium-lithium alloy saucers are exhausted of all air, creating a high vacuum inside. The bottom saucer is dish-shaped, facing the earth. So that the saucers cannot collapse, they are strengthened inside with strong struts. The atolumes measure 300 feet in diameter. The vacuum saucer structure—now weighing much less than air—rises into the sky like a balloon.** To keep the structure from rising too high, six or more strongly anchored piano wires hold it up permanently.

Normally, the structure floats from 300 to 1,000 feet up, depending upon how large an area is to be illuminated. The dish-shaped surface, which is a highly mirrored reflector, also holds several hundred or more cold fluoratomic lights. These give off no heat but supply several million candlepower per lamp. The piano wires that keep the atolumes up also conduct the required electric current to the bank of lamps. The electric energy per lamp is modest because the action is chiefly atomic.

The atolume is designed aerodynamically in such a manner that even storms of 100 miles per hour do not affect it. Normally it stays up for about a year, then it can be hauled down to renew its vacuum and its fluoratomic lamps.

*Atolume—from *atom* plus lumen = light.

**The metal shells, built like modern airplane wings, are welded. They are about 1/8″ thick. The weight of the pumped out air is about 186,500 lbs. The shells with struts weigh about 175,000 lbs. This gives a buoyancy of 11,500 lbs., sufficient to lift the lamps and float the whole structure and keep it up.

That night several atolumes had been turned on to illuminate the entire park because of the usual Sunday evening summer concert. But the concert never started.

At 2031 (8:31 P.M. Eastern Daylight Saving Time), three 10-Balls suddenly appeared over the park's vast "Sheep Meadow," their purple tubes reaching all the way down to the grass. A minute later they had departed up into the gathering twilight, and it was noted by thousands of observers that they moved far faster than they ever had on earth.

The Xenos had never visited Central Park before; what were they up to now? The answer came quickly.

THE XENOS HAD DEPOSITED OVER 200 OF WHAT APPEARED TO BE THREE-YEAR-OLD CHILDREN ON THE GRASS!

The few policemen who quickly ran to the spot had their hands full keeping curiosity seekers away; soon the crush of thousands of New Yorkers would become serious. The police ordered a number of husky volunteers to help them form a cordon surrounding the children until reinforcements from the nearby police station could arrive.

The strange-looking youngsters with their enormous, luminiferous eyes stood or sat quite placidly on the grass, conversing in monotones among themselves. The overhead atolume light seemed to bother them more than anything and they shielded their eyes with their hands to keep from blinking almost continuously.

Their mannerisms were certainly not that of three-year-olds, even though size and weight indicated that age. Their facial expressions were, to put it mildly, very mature. They eyed their cordon amusedly, yet with condescension. When the men pressed too close, they waved them away with an annoyed wave of the hand that could not be denied. So far the police and bystanders had been too amazed by these over-adult children to utter a single word to them. A solemn hush had fallen over the bystanders outside the cordon; all kept craning their necks and staring at the strange spectacle, sensing that here they had to do with some extraordinary form of life.

The children were attired only in a single piece of "clothing," similar to a nightgown. It came down to their feet, with sleeves only to the elbows.

On their upper arms there was a wide, bluish, metal-like band that appeared to glow.

The odd material of their tunics had never been seen before. It, too, seemed metallic because it reflected the light, but it looked softer and more pliable than silk.

Finally, one of the men in the cordon—it turned out later that he was a teacher—addressed the nearest child, who happened to be a girl.

"What's your name, sweetheart?"

"Sweetheart?" she asked pertly, lifting her eyebrows as if resenting the familiarity. "Davenport . . . is . . . my . . . name!" She enunciated this in a curiously accented, staccato English.

"Very good," said the teacher. "My name is Arnold Depeyster. What is your first name?"

"First . . . name?" she tittered. "One . . . enough. See?"

With that she held up her arm, encircled with the arm-band, for inspection. Depeyster bent down to read the strange, embossed inscription:

A.Z. DAVENPORT-NEW YORK-1996-30-9

"Oh," said the amazed teacher, "you were born last year on September 30 and you are the daughter of Mr. and Mrs. A. Z. Davenport of New York!"

"Evi . . . dent . . . ly," replied the little miss with aplomb and finality, turning her head away in annoyance.

Teacher Depeyster now knew what to do. With an

authoritative air, he addressed one of the police captains, asking him to record all the children's names. Then assuming his best classroom manner, he spoke to them:

"Children, it is very important to the authorities that we know your full identity so your parents can be notified immediately. Please take turns and tell us your names."

The children, sensing that they had now been placed on an adult level, cheerfully and smilingly complied. Within minutes, the information had been obtained and recorded by the police, and then broadcast forthwith.

Among the spectators had been Dubois' secretary, Miss Mary Windber. When the name of D. Dubois came up, she realized immediately that it was Duke Dubois' son. She instantly ran to the nearest visiphone and gave him the news.

She was waiting for Dr. and Mrs. Dubois on the mall as they flew in excitedly within fifteen minutes of her call. They were among the first parents to reach the cordon.

Identification was unnecessary, as everybody knew them by sight. One of the police captains lifted up their boy, who was not in the least ruffled, and placed him in the arms of his mother, who immediatedly inundated him with kisses.

The child, who had never touched a live human until that evening, was puzzled by the unaccustomed affection, but took it in his stride.

"And what is your name?" asked the new mother, tears streaming down her face.

"Dubois . . . of . . . course," said the child with an arched brow.

At this juncture, Duke Dubois, who had been looking at the arm-band with a most puzzled air, said:

"Donny, dear, our child evidently *has* no first name. That is something the Xenos were not interested in. When hatching a brood of chickens, no one would give them first names. They would naturally be banded for identification, to trace their genetic strain and other breeding information. We will name our son soon enough."

Donny nodded in understanding. Now in possession of her child—her firstborn—she was overflowing with gratitude and happiness. Nothing mattered now, not even the miracle of her son's ectogenetic birth, which occurred on Sept. 28, *three months after he was conceived!* Now less than eight months old, he was as grown up physically as a three and one-half-year-old, and he had the mentality of a completely mature adult.

While they flew back home with their precious acquisition, Dubois, Jr., took to the new experience as if he had done it all his life.

"Just . . . as . . . we . . . saw . . . on . . . te . . . le . . . vi . . . sion," was his only comment.

Papa Dubois was still puzzled.

"Who, my boy, taught you how to speak?"

The child looked surprisedly at his father.

"We . . . always . . . had . . . te . . . le . . . vi . . . sion . . . and . . . radio . . . all . . . children . . . lis . . . tened," staccatoed the boy. "Also . . . we . . . all . . . learned . . . *espanol* . . . from . . . Cuban . . . stations."

"I should have known," said Dubois to Donny. "All this came so suddenly, we just were not prepared for the too obvious."

But when they landed on the fully lit top of their villa, curiosity got the better of Dubois—he inspected his son's head, just under the hairline of the forehead.

"As I suspected," said he. "No punctures—his new heredity is 'inbuilt'!"

* * *

Scenes similar to the one in New York's Central Park

occurred simultaneously in the Bronx, on Long Island, in fact all over the world on that memorable date—*X-Day,* as it became known thereafter—the end of the Xeno occupation.

Nearly 200,000 ectogenetic "10-Ball-born" children had been left behind—abandoned, so to speak—in the obviously hurried departure of the Xenos.

Human scientists had reasoned that the Xenos were certain to transport everything, including 10-Balls and their entire contents, to Eros after they stay on our world.

But within one hour after they had left the planet, the observer team on Eros signaled the news that the two large 10-Ball construction teams had departed hurriedly, too! This team had been working on a new project—a huge 600-foot diameter dome—near the spherical-pyramid tower.

The steel or iron dome had been less than two-thirds finished and the Xenos had left so precipitously that the unsupported top of the dome had sagged badly.

Usually the Xeno engineers fashioned the native Eros iron while it was heated to incandescence. This our observers had noted when Eros dipped into the earth's shadow during the planetoid's night. Then the exposed metal of their construction projects glowed dull red for some time.

After the Xenos had gone, our men flew over the dome, coming to within a few feet of it. They noted the deep sagging of the metal and the searing heat from the still red-hot iron.

They decided that the unprecedented flight of the Xenos must have had an extraordinarily compelling reason behind it.

Scientists, laymen, indeed all humanity were vastly puzzled over the sudden turn of events. Everyone sensed that this was the end of the invasion—at least for the time being. Speculation was naturally rife about whether there was to be a later, or second invasion, but no one took such a prospect seriously. The long-awaited X-Day had come and the world was in a mood for celebrating as it never had before.

But another, far more stirring event was to chill the world first and shake it to its very foundations.

*   *   *

When Duke and Donny arrived home with their new son, they spent many hours, far into the night, becoming acquainted with him.

The super-intelligence of their youngster was so extraordinary that it overwhelmed them continuously.

From the first, the child showed a very clear understanding of his origin. The concept that he had "parents"—entities like himself—seemed elementary to him.

As long as he could remember, he and a group of other children—a little more than seventy-five—had been together in a large place where they slept, ate and lived. The light always was dim—"didn't . . . hurt . . . my . . . eyes . . . as . . . in . . . that . . . park."

They always had machines—he pronounced it *mah . . . sheens*—who attended to all their wants. These obviously were robots, since the Xenos themselves disliked high-pressure air rooms, in which they had to wear their own low-pressure suits.

The children could only remember a few rare and fleeting visits of the Xeno scientists themselves, "who . . . had . . . enor . . . mous . . . green . . . eyes." "They" were always in a "wheeled box," their heads encased in a globe at the top of the "box."

Dubois concluded that the Xenos had decided to bring up their experimental broods strictly as humans. That meant that the children not only lived in their own normal human atmosphere, but in their own full gravity.

This was contrary to the Xeno's customary surroundings, hence they could only move around in a wheeled box if they didn't wish to crumple up because of the—to them—excessive gravity.

"Look at it this way, Donny," said Duke. "Suppose you wished to visit some specimen of the deep sea fish far down in the ocean. How would you proceed?

"You could not possibly live several miles below the ocean's surface—where the pressure is tons per square inch—unless you wore a suitable 'pressure box' that surrounded your body constantly. Your head could conceivably stick out of the box, if it was encased in a heavy transparent globe. To move around on the ocean floor, your box would have to have caterpillar-geared tractors. Your arms and hands would have to be enclosed in proper flexible metal tubing to move them. Both head and arm gears would have to be *perfectly* watertight, otherwise the heavy pressured water would drown you in seconds.

"Exactly so with the children-visiting Xenos—in earth-gravity and dense terrestrial atmosphere, the superminds were completely out of their normal elements, hence they used robots whenever they could."

Dubois, Jr., nodded his head vigorously at this illustration.

The "robot-mahsheens" were good "loving" nurses, too. They fed the young infants and did everything a human nurse would do to make them comfortable.

But they never bathed them. Indeed, young Dubois did not know the term, except as it applied to grownups swimming in a pool or ocean. It developed that neither he—nor the other children—had ever been immersed in water. Evidently water was too scarce, or the Xenos did not believe in bathing.

Instead, once every twenty hours—there was no night or day in the 10-Balls—the children were "pick-picked." This is the term the youngsters used among themselves.

(The nurses spoke the language of whatever country the 10-Balls were stationed at. Thus, over the U.S., they spoke an accented English, over France, a like French, and so on. The nurses never invented words, but were fed the appropriate language by the Xeno researchers, or else language machines.)

Pick-pick went somewhat like this. The children—before they could walk—were held by their feet, head down, into a transparent cylinder. Immediately they would squeal delightedly from the vigorous "pick-picking," or body tingling, which lasted about a minute.

A blast of moist hot air accompanied the tingling sensation. The infant emerged from the cylinder red as a beet.

Dubois translated this procedure as an advanced electronic bath of some sort. It probably was a pulsating but harmless ultra-high frequency Tesla current treatment that, together with the moist air blast, removed all foreign particles, dirt, dead skin and so forth, from the body's surface, leaving it clean and free of germs.

As soon as the children could walk, they were made to stand up in the pick-pick cylinder, turn it on and remain until an automatic device turned it off. They liked it immensely, far more than the "messy . . . bath" they later had to become accustomed to.

When the children went to sleep, they didn't go to their

beds—because there weren't any, strictly speaking. Instead, they slept on curious metalloid sheets, suspended between stout metal rods. There were eight sheets in tier-like shelves, all separated about two feet. The children were "shot" by means of an inclined tube onto their sheets. They couldn't fall out of the flat bed sheets, since these had ten-inch-high sides of the same material. The supporting rods at the foot and head of the bed sheet prevented a child from falling in that direction, also.

The metalloid sheet was thick and could not sag, hence the child was always sleeping on a flat, horizontal surface.

Since the metalloid sheet was a fair conductor, it could be heated electrically, probably by a very low voltage current. For that reason there was nothing resembling a blanket or covers. The children slept comfortably in their one-piece tunic, in a fully air-conditioned hall.

If a child had to get up at night—or after sleep period—he crawled into his tube slide, which could be reversed for that purpose, and slid down.

Under questioning, it developed that none of the children had ever had a cold. Indeed, Dubois, Jr., did not understand the term.

"Evidently," said his father to Donny, "the Xenos had either found the means to inoculate the children against colds and other infantile diseases, or, what is more likely, had discovered a way to influence the human parent male sperm and the female egg—before or after impregnation—so that a young child would not be subject to any of the common children's diseases."

Indeed, the Dubois boy did not know any child who had been sick or ill, except through accidents,

Incidentally, Dubois found out that the children had no special name for the almost invisible Xenos—among themselves their hosts were known merely as *he* or *she* or *they*. They did, however, have a pet name for their nurses, who, being robots, looked exactly alike. They called them *Mahshie*. The term stems from their pronunciation of machine. The nurses also gave cuddly toys to the youngsters. These were always stuffed human forms, made of the same material as their dresses—the extremely soft and pliable metalloid cloth. These toys were mechanical, too. If one pressed their backs, they would move their heads and limbs in a certain consecutive manner, then they would hum a little song, always without words. Dubois, Jr., remembered a few of them, which his father recorded on tape.

Later research ascertained that none of these tunes were known on earth. Musical specialists recorded a total of forty-nine such distinct compositions from nearly 4,000 10-Ball-born children. The conclusion, after many months of research: *the music was extremely melodious and pure Xenian.*

Most of the youngsters took these human dolls to bed with them and nearly always fell asleep quickly while listening to the more or less repetitive musical strains.

After a light breakfast consisting mostly of somewhat sweet-tasting thick liquids, the children took various exercises, romping and running. Then they listened to the radio, which had been installed in the great hall.

This, however, was a different type of radio, which the Xenos themselves called *interpretive radio*. The original transmission usually came from a local radio station. Thus, if a particular 10-Ball was stationed near Dallas, Texas, or near Bangkok, Thailand, it would come from that city. Once a week or so, however, the transmission came from a specially selected foreign station. It seems the Xenos wanted their charges to be bilingual, for a better rounding out of the youngsters' education. French children thus learned German and vice versa, English children learned Italian, Russians learned English or Chinese (depending on where the 10-Ball was stationed) and so forth.

Interpretive radio was in reality expanded radio reception and it sounded somewhat like a slowly revolving record. The Xenos no doubt made recordings of many outstanding radio programs, but they were never played back at the original speed. They were probably recorded electronically, but not on tape.*

The underlying reason for this slow effect certainly was that young children, who as yet were not too familiar with the language, had to be taught slowly. That is why teachers the world over talk measuredly and distinctly when instructing youngsters. This fact had not escaped the Xeno language specialists. Hence, interpretive radio.

And this, incidentally, was the reason for the "10-Ball-born" youngsters' slow, staccato-like detached speech pattern, with its slight pauses between successive words.

After lunch, the children usually had a television session to familiarize themselves with human manners and behavior. The programs here, too, were evidently specially selected for youngsters. They might be network or local transmissions, or from foreign sources. However, they, like their counterpart radio emissions, were expanded interpretive television programs, too. This caused the television action to unroll somewhat in slow motion.

Both radio and television performances were always prefaced with an obviously Xenian introduction that stated: "The . . . program . . . that . . . follows . . . has . . .

*Technical Footnote: As Dubois and other scientists quickly ascertained, if there had been slowed-down tape recordings, the pitch of the emissions would have been lowered considerably, which the children would have noted quickly, too, when listening to normal earth emission. Hence, the Xenos must have used "stretched out" or expanded electronic, non-mechanical, stored recording.

been . . . slowed . . . down . . . somewhat . . . so . . . that . . . you . . . can . . . follow . . . it . . . without . . . strain."

It was natural then that when the children finally were united with their parents on earth, they became confused at first by their elders' speech pattern. On radio and television, too, the speech was much too fast for them. This was especially true of Latin and Latin-American children, where all normal speech patterns are extra rapid.

Speech experts, however, pointed out quickly that this was only a transitional condition—the children would soon accommodate themselves to normal speech practice.

As was to be expected, a large percentage of people in every country did not accept the banding of their child as conclusive, hence tens of thousands of parents wanted to make certain that no mistake had been made.

The skeptics underwent the now perfected electronic parentality test, which analyzes the parents' blood and gene types and matches these with that of the corresponding blood-gene types of the child.

Several weeks later, a special worldwide medical report confirmed that there had not been a single case of mistaken identity of any of the "10-B" children," as the 10-Ball-born were known thereafter.

Before these tests occurred, there had also been millions of scoffers, who could not bring themselves to believe that there could be tens of thousands of four-months'-premature births of children who, less than eight months later, could have reached the physical development of three and one-half-year-old children.

The press and television quickly pointed out through leading scientists and geneticists that four-month births were quite common now and that few of these prematurities have been lost since 1988, due mainly to accelerated growth techniques.

It was certain, the scientists pointed out, that the four-months' infants were already fully developed, thanks to the Xeno technicians. The prevailing scientific opinion was that the Xenos had found ways to influence the pituitary gland right at conception. This is the human gland that regulates growth. That plus additional hormone and perhaps other as yet unknown means accelerated the growth of the unborn child to such an extent that the four-month gestation in reality corresponded to the usual nine-month term.

It now seems positive that these newborn *Ultra-Humans* (as they are also called) surpassed by far the normal newborn—at birth they probably compared well with a one-year-old.

One should therefore not be surprised that an eight-month-old ultra-human child appeared like a three and one-half or four-year-old terrestrial youngster.

It also would seem that these new children will most likely be fully matured at age ten, or perhaps less.

Dr. Dubois—as well as several hundred other scientists—did his utmost to elicit from the children more information about the appearance and personality of the Xenos themselves. This, however, proved a complete failure. The 10-B children hadn't seen any more than the two metal-braced humans had observed many months previous.

Extremely frustrating as it was for science as well as for everyone, it appeared more and more likely that the true identity of the Xenos would never be known to humanity—no one could ever have a clear picture, or even a rough sketch of a living Xeno.

Said Duke to his wife, when he finally became convinced that science would perhaps never be able to solve the riddle of the Xeno race:

"We must console ourselves with the thought that there are countless familiar things we have never seen, either.

"No one has ever seen an electron or an atom, nor an electric current. We have never seen space, nor have we seen magnetism or gravitation. We have as yet to see a human thought, or the substance that is responsible for life itself. So we must add the Xenos to our long list of unidentifiable objects. Our own ultra-children in time may unravel many of our present mysteries."

13

ANNIHILATION

The lifting of the earth's siege by the Xenos occurred on the evening of June 17, 1997, at approximately 2046 (8:46 P.M. New York Eastern Daylight Saving Time). This was immediately after the invaders had deposited their *"ectoxenic"*—the Xeno artificially bred human ultra-children—on various open spots all over the world, and at about the same local time.

The radio and television as well as the cosmivoice continued to give bulletins for hours. By midnight it had been ascertained that exactly 198,749 ectoxenic children had been left behind by the departing invaders. These ultra-children, born and raised artifically by the Xenos, had all been restored without a single mishap to their own parents, who had never laid eyes on them before.

Never in the history of the world had there occurred an event even remotely comparable to the present one, where such a vast crop of an artificially bred *superrace* had appeared simultaneously on earth, with such a staggering effect on the future of humanity.

As was to be expected, the world's press had a field day next morning, June 18, the day after the "liberation" of the world. Here are just a few random excerpts from editorials of that day.

From the New York *Times:*

358 Pregnant Days

The world would be wise not to take lightly the extraordinary lessons learned by humanity during the 358-day occupation of the earth by our mysterious, still unknown invaders.

Mankind will always look back with mixed feelings on the occupation by the so-called Xenos, who, we have many reasons to believe, were definitely extra-terrestrial and certainly non-human.

On the whole, we are convinced that history will accord them the high place they deserve in the future development of world progress. Indeed, it may well turn out to be the turning point of humanity's heartbreak road, if we but heed the directions of these 358 eventful days.

It is yet too early to appraise fully the Xenian occupation, but already a number of outstanding points are clearly in evidence. We shall enumerate these briefly:

1. The occupation—if it did nothing else—demonstrated that all the nations *could* work together, for the benefit of the world. There was no strife, no wars, not even serious war talk during these 358 days. Credit the Xenos with this super achievement. To the everlasting shame of our great nations, it appears that we are still motivated by an archaic *force majeure* that can govern us, instead of ourselves governing the world peacefully.

2. The occupation evidently was, for the most part, a scientific research expedition, where one highly intelligent and superior older race investigated a much younger, far less

civilized one.

3. The occupation of the earth was not one of exploitation of the human race. On the contrary, it was beneficial in many ways—humanity stands to gain more than it gave.

4. The Xenos, by creating a new race of nearly 200,000 ultra-humans, have left us a nucleus of a new and superior civilization that is certain to revolutionize the world of the future.

5. In addition, by grafting two new important glands into 188 million of the world's young children, they have guaranteed that the future of humanity will be in safe hands—always presuming that our present-day politicians can be restrained for the next twenty years from instigating planet-wide nuclear hara-kiri. Indeed, thoughtful people might wish, for the ultimate peace of the world, that the Xenos had extended their occupation for a few decades, or at least until we had grown up sufficiently to outlaw and destroy our glorious yet tiresome atomic firecrackers.

6. Quite seriously, all nations should erect monuments to the memory of the august Xenos, who by their good example have taught the human race how to govern beneficiently and selflessly.

Bon Voyage, Xenos, mission well done!

From the Paris *Figaro:*

Have They Departed?

We would be the first to shout *Bravo!* if we were convinced that the Xenos had departed and that their *adieux* were sincere. Let us advocate patience and be certain that our former conquerors have not flown to the moon for a short summer vacation! Perhaps the heavy influx of tourists on our shores has frightened them away!

France has been invaded so often in our past history that it behooves our *compatriotes* to be cautious and make absolutely certain that here we have not to do with a return engagement of the Xenos in the near future.

The world, we know, will celebrate our erstwhile invaders' departure, when and if the fact has become official.

Far be it for us to belittle their most examplary behavior during the occupation, as well as their *formidable* deeds in the betterment of humanity. And for once we hope that our old French proverb, *"Plus ça change, plus c'est la même chose"** will be completely wrong with regard to our new generation.

In this spirit we salute you, *les* Xenos and lift our glasses to you—but please don't come back!

From the Moscow *Pravda:*

Why the Sudden Flight?

The West, we know, is greatly puzzled over the precipitate departure of the shameless invaders who made us uncomfortable at times during the past year.

It will come as a surprise to the capitalistic countries that our great inventors and engineers of the U.S.S.R. perfected a new super-weapon that would have been certain to bring down any of the clumsy 10-Balls of the odious insect race, had they stayed on another month.

There is a strong possibility that their spies discovered that several hundred of our secret weapons were being made ready in a number of our underground arsenals.

This we know today is the real reason for their sudden flight.

Let the West understand that the U.S.S.R. will not be trifled with for long from *any* quarter.

* * *

When Dubois, Jr., had finally gone to sleep on that eventful first evening of his arrival on earth, Duke and Donny spent part of the night choosing an appropriate name for their firstborn.

Inasmuch as it seemed certain that they would have remained childless if it had not been for the Xenos, they decided that the most logical name for the boy should be *Xenor,* in honor of the Xenos. Not surprisingly, thousands of other heretofore childless couples the world over were imbued with similar sentiments, hence the names Xenor, Xenion, Xendor and Xendrew for boys, and Xena, Xenia

---

*"The more it changes, the more it remains the same."

or Xenita for girls, are very common nowadays among our ultra-children.

Duke called his laboratory early in the morning, informing his secretary that he would not be in his office for the week—he and Donny were not only going to celebrate the arrival of their new son, but they were going to celebrate the departure of the Xenos at the same time.

Most of the world, that Monday morning, was in a celebrating mood. Work was out of the question—everyone had plans for a protracted holiday. Visiphones were choked with traffic of the merrymakers, making dates with friends and relatives.

Since 8:00 A.M. Donny and Duke had been busy on the visiphone, introducing their new son to all their relatives—mere friends could wait. As the Dubois' had a long list of relatives, group visiphone connections were made so that some fifty-odd calls went out simultaneously. In such connections—called *roundmultiplex circuit*—the caller is the only one who speaks and is seen. His picture and the sound of his voice are the only ones transmitted. Thus the caller can speak and be seen by any number of people on the same circuit, but the *callees* cannot be seen or heard. This saves a vast amount of time.

Little Xenor, too, had given a good account of himself, and because he spoke slowly and articulately—not like a three-year-old, but like a grownup—all his listeners were speechless in amazement, as they later reported.

Breakfast, served promptly at 8:30 by the butler, posed no difficulty for the youngster. He ate everything, but was vastly puzzled by the various eating utensils. He had never held a fork or a spoon in his hands—aboard the 10-Ball, one just drank out of cuplike objects or bottles. Most food was liquid, but there was a sort of pale-green rubbery "bread"—or was it bread? Xenor did not know its nature—the children called it *Eatit*. As time went by, he was never to taste anything like it again.

Donny was in the midst of serving a cup of hot chocolate to her son when the cosmivoice suddenly blared out urgently with extra loud volume.

The time was 8:42 A.M.

The date, June 18, 1997.

The resonant voice was that of the most celebrated reporter in the English-speaking world, Rex Renault. That broadcast was to go down in history as the greatest of the century. Fortunately, having been recorded, it is still being played back in all its stark drama, its terror and its tragedy—and it will continue to be heard for hundreds of years. Fortunately, too, a *visirecord* was made at the scene, preserved for all time.

The instant Rex Renault's voice came on, Duke switched on his wall teleprojector, so Donny, Xenor and he could watch the proceedings as they unrolled.

The cosmivoice sounded agitated from the start:

"PRE-FLASH—VISICAST FROM THE MOON—OVER 1,600 10-BALLS MASSED—REX RENAULT REPORTING—HISTORY IN THE MAKING."

Then, after a short pause.:

"Three days ago, science intelligence informed earth that the Xenos at the lunar mine had suddenly stopped transmitting lunium charged waves to their home planet. This being important news, I was commanded to take charge of a special scientific mission and make a full report. Three of Dr. Dubois' scientists, our pilot, a technician and I arrived here on the moon last night.

"We were none too early. En route, we learned that over 1,600 10-Balls, moonbound, had quit the earth Sunday evening. All had preceded us by hours.

"Commander William X. McLean, radiophoning from

the moon, had warned us not to land at our American military post, which, in view of the massed 10-Balls overhead, seemed too vulnerable. All American and Russian forces were evacuated last night and are now at the French and English bases.

"Our own spaceship rests on the peak of a 14,000-foot lunar mountain. As you can see on your *visiscreens,* the entire Xeno expedition is spread out below us in a vast but tight semicircle. They are hovering immobile about a mile from the fabulous lunium mine. Observe that Dr. Jean Pickard, our physicist, has an arrow pointing to the mine at the right corner of the screen. Note the earth at the far left.

"The Xenos have been hovering for hours in their present position. You will see that in the center there are thirteen of the much larger 10-Balls . . . . Look . . . suddenly the entire congregation of machines seems to have become enshrouded in a green mist that extends about a mile in all directions from the 10-Balls!

"Dr. Pickard, what do you make of it?"
Pause.
"Dr. Pickard thinks it is a radiation effect of some sort—he cannot be certain.

"What is the purpose of the Xenos' massed 10-Balls? Are they waiting—if so, for what? Has something gone wrong at the mine? Will there be a nuclear explosion and are they there to prevent it?

"The panorama before us is breathless in its beauty—the great mass os sparkling, silvery machines that stood out sharply etched against the dark moonside a few minutes ago is now softly bathed in a greenish mist that seems to pulsate like a living thing—note that it waxes and wanes at times—now it throbs—it is frightening, and sinister, somehow. I wish I could tell you what it all means.

"Have you noticed how far down the purple center-tubes

of the 10-Balls reach? On earth, they never seemed to lengthen more than a thousand feet or so—here on the moon they extend at least 4,000 or 5,000 feet. Is this because the 10-Balls are in their normal vacuum, or because the gravity is so much weaker here?

"While I was talking, you witnessed a sudden change. That large 10-Ball—it must be twice as large as the others—suddenly rose above the mist from its center position. Is this the leader, the commander, or what . . . ?

"Heavens, what now! Look. . . ."

Rex shouted excitedly: "Overhead, a fearful array of newcomers have just come into sight—over a dozen huge machines advancing toward the Xenos' center . . . they are vast, ponderous *spike-balls*, each at least 250 feet across. From the equator of each big sphere there extend six spikes, about fifty feet long. Near the end of the spikes are round discs. At the top of the sphere is a much taller 'conning tower' of some sort—it looks like a giant mushroom.

"The color of the big machines is copper red—now they are arranging themselves into a huge V-formation, pointing at the center of the Xenos. They move slowly and deliberately—you can see all sixteen of them, now—a terribly menacing sight. See, they have stopped moving, the two forces are about two miles away from each other as far as I can judge.

"Look . . . suddenly a cobalt-blue mist or emanation is flowing out from every spike into all directions. . . . This intense blue color reminds me of an atomic generator below water, when in operation.

"Now the blue mist is enveloping all sixteen spike-ball spaceships, like a vast blue cloud.

"Is this huge array of machines assembled here on the moon for a test of strength?

"Are the spike-balls anti-Xenian? Are they on a higher or less advanced civilization? Do they come from the same planet? Do the two forces belong to the identical insect race? How can a mere human tell?

"At the moment, nothing moves, not even the Xenos' green mist. . . . As I look at the two fleets, one which has more than 1,600 ships, the other a mere 16, I have the feeling that the Xenian armada is more sophisticated, far more elegant and more powerful.

"The spike-balls seem lumbering, slower and far less advanced.

"It is certain that at the moment some sort of communication must be going on between the two forces. What are they debating?

"How silly of me—it *must* be about the lunium mine! That's why the Xenos straddle it squarely.

"Evidently the spike-balls learned that the Xenos were sending the very rare lunium home—they followed the radiation beam to its source—and now they are here to obtain the priceless element themselves.

"Dr. Pickard just handed me a note suggesting that the Xenos probably use the lunium for the propulsion of their 10-Balls. They doubtless have a large stockpile of the extremely scarce element right here at the mine.

"But they had to leave the earth in great haste when their intelligence scouts reported the spike-balls were heading earth- and moonward.

"It seems to me that the newcomers are out to wrest their share of the vital lunium. Will the Xenos allow them to share it with them? Or will there be a battle—or an Armageddon?

"I cannot believe that, knowing how peace-loving the Xenos are—did they not implant something akin to a peace-organ into millions of our children's forebrains?

"But what about the spike-balls? What are *their* intentions? As we know nothing about them, we must remain in the dark for the moment.

"This, too, brings up the question of how many—shall we say persons, or beings—are there in the two opposing factions?

"Various guesses have been made in the past as to the Xeno 10-Ball population—they ran from 25,000 to 50,000. At the higher figure, this means over 35 Xenos per ship, but there may well be 75 per ship, or over 100,000 Xenos—a total that seems not too high in view of the vast new city they constructed on Eros, which could accommodate more than five times that many.

"As for the huge spike-balls, a 250-foot sphere could easily hold 10,000 beings with a great deal of room to spare, according to a note just handed to me by our mathematician, Dr. Pablo Munoz. That means 160,000 for all 16 machines, or well over 250,000—can we call them souls?—for both opponents . . . .

"Look . . . now we are having some action. The blue mist of the copper-colored spheres is spreading slowly toward the Xenos—they retreat slightly, now the blue mist almost touches the green emanation of the Xenos. . . .

"LORD, WHAT HAPPENED? SUDDENLY I AM BLIND!"

"This is Dr. Jean Pickard speaking. Rex Renault is temporarily blinded, but I think he will be able to go on in a minute. I had my back turned to the three-inch thick quartzite window when the frightful cataclysm occurred. I was watching the advancing spike-balls on our monitor TV, just as you did on your own screen, when, as the blue mist touched the Xenos' green emanation, there was a sudden, excruciatingly intense lightburst that filled our entire cabin with an unbearably violent illumination. A moment later, a searing hot heat-radiation wave struck our ship and almost ignited it. Fortunately we were three miles distant from the Brobdingnagian holocaust, otherwise we would not be here to tell about it.

"*The entire action was over in perhaps less than a billionth of a second. The nuclear radiation was so intense that all our quartzite observation windows turned an amethyst violet.* All of us would have been totally blinded had not the radiation struck our thick quartzite windows *first,* discoloring them in less than a millionth of a second, and saving our eyesight simultaneously.

"Because of the intense radiation, I immediately ordered our ship to rise several miles over the lunium mine, and you see it now in the center of your screen—in a violet color. Everything you view on the moon looks violet on your color visiscreen because we have no means to restore the original transparency to our windows—but here is Rex."

"THIS IS WHAT HAPPENED, ACCORDING TO MY SCIENCE CONFRÈRES:

"IT APPEARS THAT THE BLUE MIST OF THE SPIKE-BALL ARMADA AND THE MACHINES THEMSELVES WERE CHARGED WITH ANTI-MATTER OR MINUS-MATTER. THE INSTANT THE TWO MISTS CONTACTED THE TWO VAST AND POWERFUL FLEETS, THEY ANNIHILATED EACH OTHER—VANISHING TOTALLY AND IRREMEDIABLY IN LESS THAN A BILLIONTH OF A SECOND! NOTHING, ABSOLUTELY NOTHING VISIBLE REMAINS OF THE TWO SUPER-FLEETS—THEY JUST ATOMIZED INTO SPACE.

"ONE QUARTER MILLION SUPER-INTELLECTS WERE WIPED OUT IN AN INCONCEIVABLY SMALL FRACTION OF A SECOND!

"EVERYTHING—MACHINES, XENOS AND ANTI-XENOS VOLATILIZED INTO RADIATION OF EVERY KIND, FROM

X-RAYS TO HEAT WAVES.

"DR. MUÑOZ IS POSITIVE THAT SEVERAL SQUARE MILES OF THE MOON—THE AMERICAN AND RUSSIAN SECTORS—WILL BE SO STRONGLY RADIOACTIVE THAT FOR YEARS TO COME NO ONE WILL BE ABLE TO SET FOOT INTO THE REGION.

"WHAT YOU HAVE JUST SEEN AND HEARD WAS WITHOUT A SHADOW OF A DOUBT THE GREATEST WAR ACTION HUMANITY HAS EVER WITNESSED.

"If you are still puzzled about what became of the two powerful space fleets, here is a note from Dr. Pickard which reminds us that matter cannot be destroyed—we can only change it or transform it. In this case, matter—that is the two fleets—changed into a variety of radiations, part of which are scattered on the moon, the rest dispersed into space.

"We will perhaps never know exactly what prompted the mass annihilation of the two contending forces.

"They may have been age-long enemies originating on the same or different planets of a distant star-system.

"It may have been a test of strength.

"The possibility exists, too, that there was an error or a mistake in judgment in carrying out a military order by one or the other side.

"Perhaps neither of the opposing sides could return to their home sites without the necessary lunium 'fuel' element. Sharing it might have stranded *both* far from their home planet. Hence, mutual suicide was the only alternative.

"Now, we also have the answer to why the Xenos abandoned all our ultra-children in such haste. In my opinion the Xenos surely wanted to take the new human Superrace with them to Eros. But they knew what was coming—they had been alerted about the spike-balls. They did not want to be encumbered with almost 200,000 children, nor did they want to sacrifice them uselessly in case of probable hostilities.

"This, then, has been the actual and *real* end of the earth's occupation. We therefore need not look for another invasion in the foreseeable future. Perhaps not for another million years—if ever."

*   *   *

It was fortunate that the United States had an observation team on Eros at the time of the Xeno evacuation—it was the only nation which had humans on the planetoid.

Within minutes of the evacuation, Washington had dispatched a number of military spaceships to Eros which took official possession of the big satellite for the U.S. The six permanent observers had already attached the Stars and Stripes hours before to the lofty ball-pyramid tower.

The military task force immediately planted our flags all over Eros. They were none too soon—the Russians arrived while one lone corner of Eros had not been staked out as yet. Thus the Russians came into possession of approximately one square mile of iron-granite "territory" at the far eastern end of our second moon.

How does a nation take possession of a piece of rock and iron—in space—measuring almost fifteen miles long, three miles thick and three miles wide? An international law promulgated in 1976 states that a nation must plant flags and maintain a permanent force *on all sides* of a satellite or planetary body if it is to acquire it permanently. If one side or surface is not occupied, any other nation acquires it. Rights extend only to the center of the satellite or planet. Russia, therefore, now owns a one-mile-square cube, one and one-half miles down, the U.S. the rest.

Within days, the U.S. decided with full backing of Congress to build the world's greatest and most elaborate astrophysical laboratory on Eros. This project had been urged on the President of the U.S. by Duke Dubois and his science board.

Dubois felt it was high time for humanity to acquire a permanent space laboratory, away from our none-too-transparent atmosphere, laden with light-impeding moisture, soot and dust. In Dubois' words:

"At last science will have a precious new tool with which to unravel many of the great riddles of the Universe, a tool that will not only emancipate humanity immensely, but will enrich us materially in every direction."

Giant telescopes, both optical and radio, were to be erected as soon as feasible. Vast laboratories in the interior of Eros, already built by the Xenos, would be used to house several hundred scientists.

Dubois also advocated that Eros should be placed into a new orbit, 22,238 miles above the earth's equator.* The reason: Eros revolves much too fast around our planet—once every hour and thirty-nine minutes. For astronomical and scientific purposes, this is not convenient, nor practical. At 22,238 miles, Eros would revolve with the earth once a day—it would be "fixed" overhead, almost motionless.

Dubois stated that the problem of moving such a large mass as Eros would not be too simple, but possible. It could not be done with sudden nuclear blasts. The force would have to be applied gradually, such as by multiple rockets, which themselves could be nuclear, but not explosive.

Dubois also suggested that in the near future the unfinished huge dome built by the Xenos be completed and

---

*Celestial mechanics makes it necessary for a "stationary" satellite to be in the same plane as the earth's equator. If it is not, then the satellite's view of the earth changes constantly—it is no longer "fixed."

made over into a super space-hotel. One entire section equipped with quartzite windows could be set aside specifically for honeymoon couples.

Another section could be built for heart patients. Because gravity is no minute, a man weighing 150 pounds on earth weighs only 2-1/2 ounces on Eros. Therefore, cardiac cases should improve rapidly, because the greatly reduced physical effort in moving so little weight while walking or moving around frees the heart of much of its work. The blood, too, which in a normal man weighs more than 13 pounds on earth, weighs practically nothing on the little moon. Hence the heart expends very little energy—it pumps an almost weightless blood.

A survey of that architectural symphony—the three-quarter-mile-high ball-pyramid tower—disclosed that all the immense spheres were almost half solid.

Moreover, scientists noted that the bottom sphere was deeply imbedded in pure granite. As the latter is a good insulator, the giant tower could be used as a communication antenna and for a variety of other electronic purposes.

*   *   *

The end of the Xeno occupation of the earth and the tragic annihilation of their super-civilization—together with its obvious political lesson—had little or no effect on The Big 5 and the rest of the world's nations.

Within weeks, the U.S., as well as the Russians, had sent aloft their permanent Space Observation Globes, popularly called *Spyeyes*.

Both the U.S. and the Russians had built these globes before the occupation and both nations' devices differed little from each other.

They measured about forty feet in diameter and had been

placed in orbit some 22,000 miles above the earth. The U.S. had three, the Russians, two. As all so-called "stationary" satellites must gravitate over the equator for best results, one of the American globes was stationed almost motionless over the Indian Ocean, east of Kenya, Africa, the other south of the Philippines over the Molucca Sea. Because Russia extends over a greater territory than the U.S., *two* observation satellites were required.

The third, a relay globe to signal its messages home, was located south of the Cape Verde Islands over the Atlantic Ocean.

The Russian's single observation globe was stationed west of the Galapagos Islands, over the Pacific Ocean. Their relay globe was east of the Gilbert Islands in the Pacific, near the International Date Line.

At some 22,000 miles above the earth, the Americans had an excellent view that took in all of Russia, while the latter could see all of continental U.S.

Because the space observation globes—the SOG's—hovered continuously over international waters, none of the two nations could reproach the other.

Their purpose, naturally, was purely military. Each globe carried a complement of from four to six technicians, and was fully equipped with optical telescopes, radar, infrared detectors and other secret gear. Their main purpose was missile watching of the potential enemy, as well as observations of troop movements, large missile and supply bases and other war activities.

At night, infrared and various radar-detecting instrumentation came into play even more intensively than during daytime. Scientists on both sides had perfected their detecting gear so efficiently that it was now impossible for either to fire an Inter-Continental Ballistic Missile (ICBM), without the other knowing it within seconds.

This gave both nations some thirty minutes' warning time for an alert, either to head off the enemy's missile or missiles or fire their own in instant retaliation—or do both.

History teaches that all implements of war have their "counter"—sooner or later. The nuclear H-missile can be countered and checkmated by a defender's H-missile, hundreds of miles above the earth—destroying both harmlessly in space, always presuming that the defense's aim is good.

Modern electronic war technique can do this if alerted in time. Hence the urgency of the two nations to send aloft their observation globes—the key to alert.

Cannot we shoot down each other's globes by ICBM's? This is most doubtful, because all globes are rocket-power-equipped. Their search radars would detect the missile almost instantly and move out of the way within seconds. *This would also constitute a war threat and an alert at the same time.*

Besides the counter-H-missile. there are others. Electronics has progressed so far that we can aim an array of radio beams of such vast power that when they intercept an enemy missile several hundred miles above the earth, the radio waves rearrange the molecules of the bomb and set it off harmlessly in space—this despite the heavy metal envelope of the missile.

Dubois contended that we would soon have radio beams that heat a missile to incandescence and blow it up far out in space. Thus, for the moment, there was a good chance of a temporary stand-off between the two antagonists—at least until a new and more sophisticated weapon came along.

As Dubois had frequently pointed out in his lectures and world-broadcasts lately:

"The Xenos and their adversaries proved that it is

*eminently possible to commit mutual suicide if one wants it
sufficiently."*

* * *

The forces for peace had not been idle since the Historic
Annihilation of the Xenos on the Moon. Hundreds of
millions of people all over the world, under the
indefatigable harassment of the 188 million anti-war-
inoculated, "punctured" ultra-children, had become
fanatic peace advocates.

Little by little, the very idea of war aroused such
extraordinary outpourings of revulsion and resentment as
the world had never experienced before.

Statesmen, the military, all were now regularly
condemned in the world press and in all the communication
channels for even veiled remarks advocating a conflict.

No government could safely publish military or
"defense" appropriations without risking immediate
censure and vilification from the world's press and the
public. Continuous pressure was brought on governments
to reduce their military forces to small-scale police forces
or "dormant military" on the famed Swiss National
Militia pattern.

So unpopular became the whole concept of war that
whenever a statesman or any other leader uttered or wrote
even a mild warlike statement, a campaign was
immediately started to question his sanity. A complete
record of the individual since his youth appeared in short
order. His school and college records were scrutinized
minutely, and his handwriting was analyzed by the
foremost experts. Nothing was left undone to discredit him
henceforth if any adverse trait showed up in the
investigation.

THE FASHION OF THE TIMES SOON DICTATED THAT
WAR ADVOCATES MUST BE DERANGED AND SHOULD BE
CONFINED TO INSTITUTIONS, NO MATTER WHAT THEIR RANK
OR STANDING.

The international press studiously pointed out that, had
there been such a world sentiment in years gone by, men
such as Napoleon or Hitler would never have come to
power, slaughtering millions of innocents.

Duke Dubois, too, had become an ardent anti-war
advocate, not only in spirit but in action. He relentlessly
pressed his associated scientists and world-affiliated science
bodies to recognize the principle set up by him, which
simply stated: "As a scientist, I pledge myself not to assist
or further war or any war implement in my future work. I
will not knowingly associate myself with any war effort of
any government."

Surprisingly, Dubois received thousands of signed
pledges from scientists from every corner of the earth,
which were promptly publicized the world over. What
impressed the nations and the populace alike was the fact
that almost every important and outstanding scientist had
joined the ranks of anti-war advocates. This was hailed as
one of the outstanding victories of the peace forces.

Once a month, Dubois addressed all the super- and ultra-
children in a visi-world broadcast. While his lectures were
chiefly directed to the 188 million new gland-grafted—as
well as Xeno-raised—youngsters, practically everyone who
could get to a visi-receiver attended. Those who could not,
participated later in a *stored visi-reception program*.

By 1990, all television receivers had been equipped with a
non-mechanical electronic stored device called *electronic-
delayer-memory*—EDM. When one wished to play back a
visi-sound recording, he had only to flip a switch which
turned on the current. The EDM then faithfully reproduced

the program as often as wanted. It could be electronically erased, as magnetic tapes were three or more decades ago.

Here is a condensation of a recent Dubois world broadcast. He began always with the phrase by which he addressed the youngsters:

MY FUTURE WORLD LEADERS

Once again it is my very honored privilege to speak to you.

I am so greatly heartened by your more than tenacious endeavor in never letting up for a second in your history-making peace crusade.

Believe me when I say with all my heart that today the world and all of us oldsters know that you will succeed in your unparalleled task of reshaping a humanity torn by war for untold ages and setting it on its righteous course of peace—a lasting peace that will never again allow the world to experience the holocaust and insanity of war.

As our famed American general, William Tecumseh Sherman said almost 120 years ago: "War at best is barbarism. . . . It is only those who have neither fired a shot nor heard the shrieks and groans of the wounded who cry aloud for blood, more vengeance, more desolation. *War is hell!*"

While it will never be possible for me to match your bulldog ardor in pursuing every imaginable avenue of peace pursuit, it may be of interest to you that my associates and I have up to last week secured over 44,000 signed pledges from scientists all over the world, renouncing war and pledging to not knowingly work on any war project hereafter. Great was our satisfaction that almost every outstanding scientist is now on your side. I congratulate you on this great success.

In the very near future, we shall try to enlist into our ranks every able engineer and technician, because after all, *it is they* today who supply the true sinews of war—without them and their know-how, modern war is impossible.

But it is you, my talented young friends, who will make possible the next and perhaps the greatest "check-mate" move in the age-old chessgame of war—*an international strike against war!* Industrial and other strikes have been common for a long time, but a spontaneous international anti-war strike with the military and their technicians refusing to bear arms against another nation—*that is your next most important step to outlaw war.*

This, to be sure, is a fervent dream we all hope will come true some day.

Yet, I am positive, if you, my young friends and future world leaders, can only hold the dogs of war and destruction immobile for a short fifteen years, until you have in fact supplanted our present war-infected leaders—if you do not let your guard down for a minute—then this dream indeed will come true and war will be relegated into the time-dungheap of the past, the burial site of all the world's most hideous nightmares.